A NIGHT AT THE SHORE

A NIGHT AT THE SHORE

TONY KNIGHTON

ISBN-13: 978-1-954841-71-0

Brash Books
PO Box 8212
Calabasas, CA 91372
www.brash-books.com

For James Patrick Hawkins

CHAPTER ONE

B uddy got in touch on a Tuesday in late September and said he had something. "It's got to be this Friday," he said, "if you're interested." Buddy dealt cards in Atlantic City. He also had a good eye and would talk to guys like me if something looked promising. "This is the kind of thing you like."

We worked it out and the next day I took Susan to Margate. I thought it was too chilly, but she lay out on the beach while I drove to Buddy's house in Ventnor. He took more than ten minutes to come outside. When he did, he pulled free a pair of Ray Bans from his black leather coat and squinted at my Honda. "Where'd you get that piece of shit?" He slipped on the sunglasses and pointed to a black Dodge Charger across the street. "Let's take mine."

"Which way am I going, Buddy?"

He took a moment and said, "Yeah, it's better you drive." Buddy consistently affected an air of indifference. "Last night was crazy." He got into my car, adjusted the seat as far back as it would go, and after he gave me directions to a town north of Atlantic City, took a phone from his jeans and returned to describing his evening. "I was partying with this cocktail waitress." I supposed his manner came from dealing with the people at his table. Or maybe he'd learned it on the corner, as a kid. He never sounded excited. "Cute little chick. Fucked me cross-eyed." He was checking box scores and muttered, *"Figlo puttana,"* but then said, "Ass like you wouldn't believe."

"Put the phone away." I didn't like the detachment because it was feigned. The bulk of his income came from moving things like jewelry. Most big fence operations were part of an organization. Being an independent, like Buddy, was dangerous. Up front, he dealt with bad people who knew he had cash. On the back end were more bad people who knew he had expensive goods. The one time I'd taken him anything, a guy holding a Mossberg pump had covered the room, but that guy was a subcontractor, not a partner. The only way Buddy could stay in business was by being more dangerous than his clientele. I said, "What are you showing me?"

He stayed quiet for a few moments, still looking at his phone, probably to be a dick, and said, "This guy, comes to the joint. Plays blackjack." He did something with the phone and slipped it into his jacket pocket. "Degenerate high roller, but one of these controlled degenerates, you know?"

I turned onto Dorset Avenue, took it across the canal and turned north. In the near distance, the casino hotels dwarfed the rest of the skyline. We passed a little airfield on the far side of the channel from us. It was windy. Buddy rolled up his window and watched his reflection in the vanity mirror as he poked at his hair. "Dude comes around every weekend." He leaned forward to inspect his results and the tiny silver cross hung around his neck swung free on its skinny chain, bouncing against his purple tee shirt on the backswing. He continued, "Every Friday and Saturday night, he comes to the joint, always buys just under ten K worth of chips. I been told he always pays in hundreds."

"Who told you that?"

"I know what you're thinking but don't worry about it." He looked at me and said, "I never asked nobody—this guy don't even sit at my table. Few weeks ago, a bunch of us were having drinks at this club we go to after work. One of the cashiers was telling us a story and mentioned him in passing, like. It's what first got me thinking about this piece of business." He looked back at his reflection in the mirror and fussed with his hair some more. Buddy wasn't a bad-looking guy, even with a nose that looked to have been broken and poorly set. "Thing is, once he's lost the ten, he never plays no more. Not one more hand." Finished with his hair, Buddy flipped the visor up and sat back. "Charlie's disciplined. That's his name—Charlie. Anyway, he's disciplined. Must be a good catholic boy. I figure he's gotta be keeping Saturday night's money at the house over Friday night. I followed him, twice, so the address is solid." Buddy took an e-cigarette from the inside pocket of his coat. "You mind?"

"Yeah. I do."

"Good Christ," he said, "you're a miserable prick," but put it away and kept on about women and cars until we were going past the hotels.

I interrupted him. "What's Charlie's last name?"

"I don't know. This cashier never called him nothing else. If he's paying for his chips with cash, she probably don't know it."

"How does he make his money?"

"How the fuck would I know?"

"That concerns me. If you don't know what he does, it means you don't know who he is."

Buddy's phone rang. He said, "So what," looked at the number and killed the call.

"You've been careless before."

"The fuck are you talking about?"

I said, "That game you put me onto? Danny Raco was one of the players."

"The card game in Longport?"

"That's the only game we talked about."

"I never heard nothing about him being there." He began cracking his knuckles. "That's just bad luck, man."

"No, he's a regular."

"Who told you that?"

"He did."

"No shit?" He sounded amused. Finished with his fingers, one at a time he pushed the heel of one hand against the palm of the other to crack his knobby wrist joints. "When'd you talk to him?"

"A few months ago."

Buddy popped an elbow and said, "Look, man—"

I said, "Stop that."

"Sorry." He brought his arms down. "I don't understand why you're complaining. As I remember, you two made a lot of money off that job."

"That's right. We did."

"All right. So, what's your point?"

I took a breath. "My point is, there are some people you don't take from. It's unprofessional to bring me a job you haven't checked out."

Without acrimony, he said, "Fuck you. I'm exposed enough following this guy home. It ain't like I can chat him up."

"You don't have to ask him."

"It would be unprofessional for me to ask *anybody* questions about a guy before he got robbed. Whoever I asked would think about me. I wouldn't like that. Neither would you."

"No, but there are ways of finding things out that don't involve exposure." I was annoyed and said, "What the fuck, Buddy? You know all this, so stop arguing with me."

Buddy stayed quiet. He might have been pissed off. I didn't care. If I was being honest with myself, I didn't really need the work, then. I suppose I was restless.

Past Harrah's, we approached a steeply arced stringer bridge that spanned a larger body of water. A small placard at the abutment read Absecon Inlet. The bridge roadway was split by a concrete median barrier and narrowed to two tight lanes in both directions with no shoulder. I looked past Buddy, out, at the ocean. It was choppy. Some gulls were flying against the wind but making little headway. They seemed almost to hover.

Buddy broke the silence. "Look, once—" He started over. "This one time, he stopped by my table, just watching, like, and this other guy he was with was asking him about zoning or taxes or something. Whatever Charlie does, he's a straight arrow. A citizen."

I'd have to check that if I could. This whole thing felt strange. Buddy could be trying to bullshit me or not, but there was something else, too. It might have been my imagination but there seemed something about Buddy's manner that I didn't remember noticing before. This was feeling more and more like something I didn't want to do but I'd come down here, and I should at least see what the job looked like. I passed a slow-moving Chevy pickup. As we neared the bridge's apex, I said, "What else do you know about him?"

Buddy's cell rang again. "He's a Guinea, like me, and he's gaudy."

"That's not helpful."

As though I hadn't spoken, he said, "Gold money clip, cigarette case, Cartier watch, shit like that, so he probably got some nice things in his house, there. Besides the ten K." Buddy pulled his phone out. "If you see anything I can move, you know? You're gonna have a lot of time." He looked at the number. "I gotta take this."

I'd had enough. "You answer that phone, I'm done."

He looked out the passenger window at the ocean and said, "Be cool, man. This'll take a second." He answered the caller. "Hey."

I'd also had enough of his corner boy bullshit and pulled into the right lane, stopped and shifted into park. I turned to him and said, "Put it away or get out of my car." I had us idled at the uppermost point of the span. The water's surface was a good seventy feet below.

"What the fuck?" Buddy seemed flustered. "This ain't cool, man." To the caller, he said, "Hang on," and turned to look at traffic behind us. "What if a cop pulls up?"

"I'll deal with it. What do you want to do?"

Cars flashed by on our left, their horns Dopplering past us. The guy in the Chevy truck yelled something as he steered around us. Buddy turned back and stared at me for a few moments, said, "I'll call you back," to the caller and made a performance of shutting down his phone. He showed me the blank screen, said, "There. Happy?" and put it away. "Can we get going now, please?"

I sat there. "It's not a matter of me being happy. It's about taking things seriously—" A tractor-trailer driver sounded his air horn behind us until a gap in traffic let him change lanes and pass. When he did, I said, "If you can't do that, I can't trust you."

Buddy's face changed, from a look of petulance to something else. "Whoa." He put a hand up and leaned back against the door. "You got the wrong idea." He still sounded pissed off but behind that, he seemed frightened. "I never crossed nobody, ever. Swear to god." He brought his tiny silver cross to his lips and kissed it.

It was curious. I said, "I'm talking about being careful and competent. Professional. I don't know what else you think I mean."

"Sorry." He didn't sound angry anymore but still looked wary of me. "I misunderstood you."

"I said exactly what I meant."

"Yeah, you did. I overreacted." He looked out the windshield and said, "You got a reputation."

I said, "I don't know anything about that," but put the car in gear and moved into traffic.

Below us, the narrow barrier island looked like any other shore town. Past the bridge, houses lined a long causeway. Boats were moored behind some. I followed the road onto the island, past a strip of businesses and drove through the little town, past a seawall and boardwalk separating the beach from houses on the island side.

There were fewer houses this far north. The street angled inland. I followed it and then took a turn back, toward the ocean and pulled over a few hundred feet from the house Buddy wanted me to see.

Only the side fronting the street was completely visible from where we parked, but it was enough to get a sense of the house. What looked like a two-car garage stood at beach-level. The rest, the upper three floors, were a massive example of modern beach construction. The house likely hadn't existed ten years before and gave an impression of impermanence. Its roof was all angles, covered with cedar shakes. It was sided with some type of composite that resembled the color of oyster shell. There was lots of glass—windows and skylights. An exterior stair led from beach-level to balconies on every floor. These wrapped around three sides of the home and incorporated a deck adjoining the smaller top floor, that faced the ocean. It all sat on concrete pilings footed in the sand.

Charlie's neighbors weren't close enough to be a problem. Across the street were a few houses with a lot of space between them. Those on his side backed up to a broad stretch of beach fronting the Atlantic Ocean. Most homes here were already closed-up for winter. Two houses from us, a crew was boarding over the windows. Intermittent flurries of *pops* from their nail guns punctuated the sounds of their compressor.

"You shouldn't have no trouble getting inside," Buddy said. "See them outdoor steps, there, going up to the deck? You can pop a window open or something—but I don't have to tell you your business."

He rolled down his window, took the vape out again and looked at me. I nodded. He took a hit, blew it out the window and said, "All these little towns empty out after the season." Buddy nodded toward the men and said, "Guys like them stick around but not many others." He took another hit and replaced the pen. "Won't be much coverage, neither. This time of year, they cut back to just the full-time cops—about half of what they have here in the summer. The baby cops go back to college or whatever it is those assholes do." The wind gusted and one of the crew fought to hold onto a sheet of particle board. Buddy said, "That shit looks like nothing but work."

I said, "His house is probably alarmed."

"You can count on it."

The garage door of Charlie's house rolled up and a white Mercedes coupe bumped onto the roadway and came in our direction. Buddy opened the console between us and looked inside. "That's him."

I pretended to look inside, too, but needn't have bothered. The man was oblivious. He seemed to be talking to himself but was likely on the phone. He wore sunglasses and had a lot of curly gray hair. When he passed, I tried to read his tag in the reflection in my side-view mirror, but he was moving too quickly and turned at the corner.

Buddy shut the console. "Real degenerate. Sucks at cards."

I'd need to try for Charlie's full name through his address. I got back on subject. "I don't know much about alarm systems."

"Don't have to. There's a storm coming up the coast, supposed to get here Friday, Friday night. They're calling for it to be bad." He pointed to the crew covering windows. "That's what's up with these dudes. Guys like them been working twelve-hour days all this week, all up and down the shore. Even in the rain we've had already. Must be amphibious. Anyway, once the storm hits, every alarm in town's gonna be going off."

"Not all of them."

The ground man used a circular saw to rip a sheet to size. Buddy spoke over the noise. "A lot of them, at least. Cops will have their hands full, anyway. Response times will go to shit. If you *do* set something off in there, the cops will probably only do a drive by and as long as they don't see nothing, just go on to the next call." He took the vape from his shirt pocket again but said, "You partner with a guy that knows alarms, don't you?"

"He's gone."

"That's too bad."

"Yeah. What about a dog?"

"No." He hit the vape. As he spoke, the wind drew his smoke out the window. "I checked that the first night I followed him. If he had a dog, he'd need to take it out for a walk once he got home. I waited around, like twenty minutes. No dog."

"The money might be in a safe."

"It might but that'll save you time. Easier to find and it won't be nothing tough like a floor safe set in the foundation, cause there ain't no foundation. If he has a safe, it's set in a wall. The biggest piece of solid lumber in that place is probably a two-by-four. A wall safe'll pop out real easy, and it'll be a tin can. You can chop a hole in the back. Or just take it with you."

"The guy might stay home if it's bad out."

"Uh-uh. That blizzard, last winter? The county closed the roads and he *still* made it in. He bullshitted his way past the cops and across the bridge. I'm telling you, he's a fiend for action. Guaranteed, the man will be playing cards this Friday night."

"You're really selling this, aren't you?"

"Selling, my ass." Buddy sat back, facing me. "This job sells itself. It's a money maker."

I thought about it. "All right." Buddy was annoying but he had a good eye and usually had good instincts. I'd always made money with him. "All right," I said. "What do I owe you?"

"Make it twenty-five hundred."

"A twenty-five per cent finder's fee? You kidding?"

"This is a cake job, and you know it."

"Then do it yourself."

He ignored that and said, "My time is worth something, man."

"Yeah, let's see, twice you went fifteen minutes out of your way after work to follow the guy. Both ways, that's what, an hour total, and today, you've taken this twenty-minute drive with me."

"I did more than that."

"Yeah, you waited around to see if he walked a dog. But not much else." I took out my roll and peeled off five one-hundred-dollar bills and held them up.

"You know, there could be way more than ten K in there."

"Nine K."

He paused and said, "Right, right, nine and change but there could be more."

I stared at him until he said, "It's not just my time, man. It's my expertise, like."

I peeled off five more. "If this isn't enough, I'll take you back to your place and you can call somebody else."

"Storm's in two days. That don't leave much time to call nobody."

I shrugged.

"All right," he said. "A thousand it is."

I handed him the bills. "Buddy, your name is written in that great book of swell guys."

While I backed the car into the cross street, Buddy wrapped the money around his own roll of bills. I said, "It looks like you're doing all right."

"Player hit a streak last night and tipped me half a stack."

"I thought you guys pooled your tips."

"Nah. That's the slots attendants and other dealers. I deal poker." He made to take out his phone and said, "You mind if I call that guy back, now?"

"You can call him when I drop you off."

"Christ, but you're a prick. Look," he paused, as if debating with himself and said, "this guy takes action, and he only calls me when he needs help covering something. This could be time-sensitive, you know?"

"I'll have you back in twenty minutes."

He said, "Prick," but settled back in his seat. Along with women and cars, he talked about Thursday night's Phillies game and the spread on this Sunday's Eagles-Giants game until I pulled over in front of his house. He said, "Hey, you need a piece? I picked up a few very nice automatics last week. A silencer, too."

"You keep swag in your house?"

"I didn't just start doing this last week, man." He sounded insulted.

"I apologize."

"They're a few blocks away, if you want to take a look."

"I only carry when I need to. I didn't start doing this last week, either."

"Fair enough. Just thought I'd ask. Like I said, you see anything nice, think of me." We shook and he got out of the car. "Later." His front steps were flanked by flowering bushes. He brought out his phone and thumbed up a number as he walked toward his front door.

I looked at the clock on my dash. Buddy had kept me nearly a half hour longer than I'd expected. I called Susan as I pulled away. "Sorry, I'm running a little late. You had enough?"

"I would have swum more if I'd known but I'm dressed now." She sounded testy. "You can take me to dinner. Somewhere nice. I want to sit outside."

"Aren't you cold? It's getting chilly."

She said, "Maybe for you, it is," and ended the call. She'd sounded like Buddy. I would have laughed if it hadn't seemed so abrupt.

The sun set across the bay as we ate. It was windy, walking to my car. Susan put her pink backpack in the trunk, and we left for home. She slid her seat forward. "Your friend must have long legs." I took Atlantic Avenue north toward the A.C. Expressway. Stars were just visible in the sky when she said, "What did he show you?"

Her question took me by surprise. She knew the kinds of things I did. I never went into detail, but she read the papers and could fill in some of the gaps for herself. Her asking me questions was different. I said, "A house." I understood her curiosity but there were other considerations. "It's best I not tell you much—"

"Yeah, I know. I don't want to be an accessory before the fact. I didn't mean that. I meant what's so special about it?"

There had been no change in affect, but it was clear that she was unhappy. Through dinner she'd been subdued. I hadn't paid attention. I'd been working, thinking about the job. I glanced at her. She looked as though she hadn't a care, staring at the highway through the windshield.

I answered. "The guy who owns it leaves a lot of money there on Friday nights."

"We're okay for money."

We were. I'd made a decent score early this summer. Susan hadn't liked it. I'd gone looking for money that people had died for. In general, though, she never commented when I told her I had something going on. I said, "You're right. I'd just like to top off the kitty. This should be an easy job."

"They're always easy." There was an edge to her voice now.

Why hadn't I seen this coming? Was she that good at hiding her feelings or had I been oblivious? I said, "What's the matter?"

"This is the matter. You ask me to do a day at the shore but it's only so you can look at something."

"Right. That's what I told you." Her feelings seemed unfocused but that might not really be the case. She could need to build up to what she was really upset about. "I said this was a work trip."

"Yeah, that's right. You did." I thought I'd made my point, but she said, "When do you plan to *do* this work?"

"Friday."

"Good. I can go to the opening myself."

"I'm sorry." How did I forget that? "This thing is time-sensitive."

"Fine."

I wouldn't have gotten involved with this had I known Susan was upset. I began to tell her I'd skip it. "Look—"

"Don't. I didn't really want to go, anyway."

I was debating with myself whether to pursue the point when she said, "There's a storm coming, but I suppose you already know that."

She was quiet, then. It would be better to talk about this later, after we'd gotten home.

Traffic was sparse, and we made good time. It wasn't until we'd driven past the Garden State Parkway exit that she said, "Melissa's father had a stroke."

"That's awful." Melissa was one of Susan's friends I'd never met. "How old a guy is he?" It was a shame for anyone, but I welcomed the change of subject.

"I'm not sure. I think he's still pretty young. She's coming home to take care of him."

I searched my memory for where she lived. "That's a lot."

"Yeah, it is. Melissa's a good person." Susan was quiet for a while, but it felt like there was more coming.

There was. She said, "She got leave but there's no telling how long she'll need to be home. The others won't be able to cover her shifts forever."

I remembered then that Melissa was her friend who lived in the U.S. Virgin Islands. Saint John. Susan hadn't changed the subject at all. I got to it. "You want to go fill in for her while she's here."

"I can sublet her place, so she doesn't lose it. I have a little vacation time saved. After that, I'll take administrative leave. You'll have to handle the month-to-month stuff with the house."

This was coming fast. "Okay."

She didn't say anything else. She'd known for a while that we were going to have this conversation.

I said, "Isn't Saint John in the path of the storm?"

"No."

We didn't talk much the rest of the way home or after. She was packing Friday afternoon, when I left for the shore.

CHAPTER TWO

When the lights winked out in Charlie's house, I reeled in my line. In the past hour, the breakers had gained intensity. I cinched the zipper on my jacket against the wind, slung my backpack over my shoulders and walked toward the house, on the hard, wet sand, just past where the waves lost momentum and drained back. The rod bounced gently with every step.

Light shown from maybe one house out of every half-dozen. Many were boarded up in anticipation of the storm. I could still hear the *pop* of nail guns in the distance—some crew working late.

Ahead, an older guy was loading things into the bed of a red Ford pickup, backed toward the water. His rod was still slid into a plastic tube, stuck there in the sand. Its line, barely visible, stretched taut from rod tip to where it disappeared, somewhere past the surf, and oscillated in the wind. As I neared, the man hoisted an Igloo cooler to the tailgate. He looked my way and said, said, "How'd you make out?" loud enough to be heard over the wind and waves.

"No luck."

"I took a few striped bass. They like the nasty weather," he paused and looked toward the sea and said, "but this my limit."

The horizon line was indistinct, sea and sky gone the same dark gray. Lightning flashed somewhere behind me, and a couple seconds later there sounded a report. A gust almost took the ballcap I'd gotten when I bought the rod and reel. I turned away and tugged on the hat's bill.

The guy lifted the lid and took a bottle of beer from the cooler. "Have one?"

I didn't want him to get a good look at me, but a show of rudeness would likely be remembered. "No," I said, "thanks, though." Better to chat for a moment. "You need any help?"

The old guy said, "Thanks, I got it." He closed the lid but kept the beer and winked at me. "Roadie." He feigned concern and said, "You're not a cop are you?"

I chuckled. "Not at all." Between a gap in the dunes, I caught a glimpse of Charlie's car, heading south. His headlights were on. So were the streetlights. "Have a good night."

"You do the same." He left the beer unopened on the tailgate, took his rod out of the tube and began reeling in his line.

I walked across the beach, took the walkway through the dunes and up the street, toward Charlie's house.

I stood on the driveway under the house and wiped off the rod. The lights of the casino hotels shown through the mist. Lightning flashed again, inland—closer, this time. Thunder sounded a moment later. I ditched the rod alongside the garage and climbed the stairs. The wind was colder, up on the deck. Twin glass sliding doors afforded me a view inside. In my penlight beam I saw a wrap-around sectional that dominated the room's center. There was a huge flat screen facing the long dimension, a flagstone fireplace, and beach art on the walls. The sliders were fitted with a first-class lock and were likely alarmed, too. Buddy was probably right about the storm setting off alarm systems, but there was no point in taking unnecessary chances.

The windows this high likely weren't wired. A dormer projected from the steeply pitched roof, five feet from the deck. I stepped over the rail. The shakes were barely walkable, but I made my way to the window, took a foot-long wrecking bar from my backpack and pried the lower sash up until it overcame the latch. I stepped over the sill and inside.

I was already upstairs, so I started there, looking behind the bad art with the penlight. Whoever decorated the house had no visual sense. Lots of bad seascapes. The furniture in the living room was expensive but all over-sized, lightweight crap. I turned over the stuffed chairs and couch sections to see if anything was fixed to the bottom. There were ashtrays on each end table—one from the local Chamber of Commerce—but they were clean—no butts or spent matches. Neither did the home smell of cigarettes. It looked as though the house was professionally cleaned.

Above the headboard in the master bedroom was a painting as broad as the bed, of driftwood on sand, strewn with kelp. Curiously, the furniture in here was different—a matching queen bed, nightstands, twin bureaus and dressing table were all Fifties Art-Deco style, in figured blond wood. It was well-built stuff, the joints all nicely dove-tailed, but searching the drawers yielded no money or anything of worth.

I found a little seven-shot Beretta Tomcat in a night-stand drawer. I took it to the master bath and put it in the toilet tank. I didn't want it, and if Charlie came home before I left, I didn't want him to have it, either.

Charlie's walk-in closet was mostly filled with good quality, conservative suits and jackets in black or gray. Most of his dress shirts were white or light blue. He had half-a-dozen pairs of expensive oxfords and wingtips, mostly in black. None of it seemed like clothes a gambler would wear but I let it go. It looked like a girlfriend stayed over some nights—there were women's clothes in his closet and odd bottles of make-up in the master bath—but it was clear that no woman lived here with him, and unlikely there'd be any jewelry. Charlie had a few pieces of his own, like matching cufflinks and tie-clasp sets, and it was all gaudy, like Buddy said it would probably be, but not worth taking.

I heard a quiet tapping sound and looked outside. It had begun to rain. The streetlight glittered through the drops on the windowpanes.

Lining the hallway were framed black and white photographs, likely newspaper photos, some decades old. They were all of groups of people, mostly men in suits. One, a yellowed eight by eleven print was of a groundbreaking ceremony on the beach. A bunch of suits wearing new, shiny hardhats emblazoned with The Flagship wore their best smiles and huddled around a fat guy ready to plunge a shovel into the sand. Behind them was a small crowd gathered near a caterer's tent. Someone with complicated handwriting had signed the picture. I made out the words, "Thanks for making this happen, Charlie." I couldn't pick out Charlie in the picture.

There wasn't anything for me in either of the third-floor bedrooms. I took the interior stairs at the end of the hall down to the second floor.

I found a door, identical to the others but its knob was locked. I thought it unlikely to be alarmed and kicked it open to reveal an office—desk, computer, swivel chair, filing cabinet. Opposite the window was a poorly executed depiction of sunrise over the waves.

Over the desk was a photo of a much younger Charlie, shaking hands with a bigger, older man. The older guy had his left hand on Charlie's shoulder and was smiling at the camera. Charlie was facing the older guy with a look of both admiration and pride. Neither man's expression seemed forced or phony. In ink, was written "Congratulations, Charlie! This is just the start, Kid." It was signed, "Hap." I realized this was the only photograph of Charlie I'd seen in the house.

There was nothing of interest in the desk drawers. The file cabinet was a few years old, but its lock looked new. I popped off its rim with an awl and punched out the cylinder.

In the moment, I felt extra-cautious. People with things to hide have been known to booby-trap cabinet drawers. I stood to the side and pushed them open with the prybar, starting with the bottom first. It opened without result, and I looked inside and found nothing but accounting files and paperwork that mostly seemed to have to do with county business. The name Charles Picozzi showed on a lot of the paperwork, and I assumed that was Charlie's full name. He was on the Atlantic County Board of Commissioners. A lot of the paperwork concerned large sums of money, but there wasn't any money in the drawer. I went through the rest of the file drawers. None were rigged, neither was there any money in them.

I kept at it, going through the second floor. The bedrooms here both seemed to be for guests and were mostly unused. I kept checking behind the bad pictures with my penlight.

The kitchen was on the floor above the garage. If Picozzi threw parties, this is where his guests would be. It was as big as any of the other rooms, laid out for someone who clearly liked to cook, but also seemed the only comfortable room in the house. Its walls were painted a deep red that worked well with the maple cabinets. A table that could seat six took a corner with windows on either side that afforded a view of the beach, and glass doors that opened onto an outdoor balcony. The countertops puzzled me, momentarily, looking almost like terrazzo, but proved to be concrete, poured and ground in place to expose its aggregate of multi-colored river stone. A heavy iron rack suspended from the ceiling was festooned with nice, copper-bottomed pots and pans that showed wear but were cared for. A bar magnet fastened to the wall held knives with oiled, wooden handles, and blades of a good quality high-carbon steel. I drew a finger against the edge of a large chef's knife; it was razor-sharp. I went through the drawers and cabinets. His China and glassware were first-class. I liked everything about the room but found no money.

A blue, cut-glass ashtray holding two crushed-out butts sat on a countertop next to an antique cedar box, inlaid with ivory and filled with cigarettes. I thought it an odd, nearly archaic detail in a modern house, and supposed that along with his gambling addiction, the man was a serious smoker. Also, on the counter stood a small birthday card. Inside, it was signed, Love, Rita. There was a lipstick-print kiss on top of the signature. Under the card was its pink envelope, addressed to Charlie Picozzi. The return on the back showed the sender's name was DiMichael, and she was local, at 4500 Brigantine Avenue.

I kept looking. The bottom of the stairs was at beach-level. Partitioned away from the long dimension of the garage was a mud room and small gym, equipped with a treadmill and a Bowflex. A thin layer of dust covered both. The inside door to the garage was ordinary but I was puzzled, until I realized this was where the alarm keypad should be but wasn't. Neither had I seen one anywhere else. Odd but I let it go.

A tiny, unframed oil of a lighthouse at dusk was hung in the hallway. It was better than anything else the man had, and I wondered why he'd stuck it here. I shifted it away from the wall and flicked on my light. Taped to its back was a five by seven Manilla envelope. I pulled it free and looked inside. There were credit cards, two New Jersey Driver's licenses, some money and what looked like two passports. I stuck it all in my backpack and kept looking.

I was in a small sitting room, mostly given over to storage, when from outside, I heard that one-note *whoop* of a siren toggled on and off to get someone's attention. I moved into the hallway. Standing back from the gymnasium window, I looked outside. A patrol wagon was stopped there, across the street. The cop was holding his radio handset, looking at his side-view mirror as a black Chrysler sedan pulled to a stop behind it. Raindrops— heavier now—showed in the headlight beams and the wipers on both vehicles were going. The driver and two guys in the back got out. They were dressed like me, dark windbreakers and work pants. The cop waved at them. The driver walked up to the cop's window and began talking to him as the Chrysler's front seat passenger got out. He was a little older than the others and wore a shirt and tie under a gray trench coat. He barely acknowledged the patrol cop, moving a hand in a perfunctory wave while looking toward the house.

I didn't wait to see what else happened. I picked up my backpack and took the interior stairs to the top floor. Glancing out a front window, I saw the cop and four plainclothesmen crossing the street toward the house. The cop was speaking on his portable. Two went toward the garage below me and the cop and other two walked around the side toward the exterior stairs. Raindrops were visible in the glare of the streetlamp.

I left the slider locked, went back out the dormer window I'd come in through and slid it shut. The shakes—now slick with rain—were treacherous but I made my way around the dormer to its far side and sat on the roof behind it. Obviously, I'd set off an alarm—maybe the office door I'd kicked in. What didn't make sense was the response. It was over-sized, even for a rich man's home. I waited, silently cursing both Buddy's carelessness and my own. Mostly, my own. Susan's plans to leave Philadelphia had taken up too much space in my head and I'd neglected to prepare for this job as I should have. I hadn't bothered to find out who Picozzi was.

I heard them come up the stairs onto the deck. They rattled the slider. One of them said something I didn't hear. Another said, "It doesn't matter how he got in. Those are clear signs somebody tossed the place. Get video, and make sure you show the disturbance." I cursed myself for not righting the furniture and heard a chirp as one keyed a radio microphone. "Yeah, Bluff, everything's locked up here, too but we got probable cause—we got evidence someone was inside, looking. You want us to make entry?"

There was another chirp, and a response I couldn't make out. The guy on the deck said, "Okay, you got it." He rattled the sliding door again and said, likely for the benefit of a recording, "I am New Jersey State Trooper James Robinson, badge number fifteen-sixteen. We are on location at one five two one East Beach

Avenue at seven-thirty-five PM, September twenty-third. There are no outward signs of forced entry, however, visible through several windows and a glass door there are clear signs of an intrusion. We are making entry to the dwelling, taking all reasonable caution to limit damage to the property." To someone on the deck the speaker said, "Go ahead."

A few seconds later, I heard someone snapping the trigger on a bump tool and there was a louder *clack* as the lock disengaged. It sounded like they slid the door open and went inside.

I pulled myself up to the top of the dormer and stole a glance at the deck. It was empty. There could be another wave of cops coming. It was time to go. I stepped across the shakes, hopped over the rail, squatted by the stairs and looked down.

The other two waited there at beach-level. A few moments later the first-floor lights came on and the cops inside unlocked the door and let them in. I started down. The interior lights would make it difficult for them to see outside.

Another patrol car pulled up as I was coming down the stairs to street level. He was local and might not know the state cops. He looked young. I waved. He waved back as he got out of the car. I walked in his direction and said, "Boss wants me to bring the van around. Go on, they'll need a hand."

He nodded and said, "You got it," as we passed each other. He sounded eager. His nametag read McCarthy and he hurried across the street to the house. He looked too young to be on the force.

I made it to the far side of his car and looked back as he was trotting up the stairs. I knelt and punctured his right rear tire with the awl. I did the same to the Chrysler and the first patrol car, too and moved on, south, in the direction of my car, cutting through a yard to the next block over.

I heard shouting from the house and looked back. One came out from the garage. The rest ran down the stairs. The kid must have mentioned me to the cops inside. Two of them took off on foot, checking around the house. Another in plainclothes hollered to one of the uniforms, "Stay back and hold the scene."

He shouted, "Nolan got it." It was the young guy.

I began moving again, glancing back at intervals. I heard the Chrysler's engine firing, and the driver banging it into gear. It pulled forward twenty feet but rocked to a stop. The driver and the older guy got out and looked. The older guy yelled, "Fuck it. Let's go."

One pointed toward the ocean and yelled, "He must have run down the beach."

The kid yelled, "*I* don't see anybody out there." He sounded annoyed.

The older guy said, "Shut up and keep looking. It's getting dark." The guy called to the others, "He's gotta be around here, somewhere. He can't be far." He and the others started away down the beach. They made a lot of noise, calling to each other, barking orders at the young guy to follow them, as they swarmed the area. They seemed pretty well organized but were quickly moving in the wrong direction, away from me.

I took the opportunity and crawled through another yard, getting myself soaked. I hopped a fence and was moving through the next yard when a security light snapped on. I got clear and kept going but heard the young guy shout, "He's over that way."

Something buzzed past my head as I heard a shot. Two more rounds followed. Someone shouted, "*Yo!*" One of the others yelled, "The fuck are you doing? Put your fucking gun away." I kept on. A house light came on at the far end of the block, and I heard a screen door scrape open somewhere.

There was a sheltered spot behind a darkened home's central air unit. I squatted there and listened to them crisscrossing the neighborhood. They were still making noise, shouting directions to each other. While I waited, it occurred to me that it was way out of line to shoot at a burglary suspect.

When I heard them pass and move into the next block, I took off. One surprised me as I came around the corner of the house, McCarthy, the young guy. He was surprised, too, and dragged at his pistol. I dove, grabbing his wrist with both hands as the gun came free of its holster, and twisted it away from him while driving my shoulder into his chest. We fell and his head smacked the concrete with an audible, *thunk.* The weapon flew from his grip and landed somewhere away from us. I readied to hit him again, but it proved needless. He was out cold, raindrops falling into his motionless eyes. I checked his pulse at the carotid. It was there. I didn't want him dead. I did want a gun, but he didn't have another, and I couldn't afford to lose time searching the tall grass. I left the Taser on his belt.

I picked up my backpack, cut to the next street over and ran. My car was the other way but if they heard it start and made me in it, I'd be screwed. I was getting winded. The backpack hit the side of my thigh with every step. I slung it over my shoulders and kept on.

I dropped to the ground as I saw between houses that two were on the next street over, moving parallel to me. I waited for them to move farther away from me, but they'd stopped, too. The guy in the trench coat held his radio close and said, "Repeat that." I couldn't make out what came over, but he said, "*Fuck.* All right, call for an ambulance and have the uniform stay with him." He paused and said, "We gotta get this guy, now. Go back and get the car." He paused and after another garbled response, said, "I know the tire's flat—I don't care if it'll fuck up the rear, bring the fucking car, Billy." He put his radio in his pocket, said to the other guy, "Jesus, he can be one dumb motherfucker, sometimes," brought out a phone and thumbed numbers into it.

The other guy said, "What happened, Bluff?"

While he waited for an answer on his phone, Bluff said, "McCarthy's kid got hurt—bad. Unresponsive."

"The fuck is he doing here, anyway?"

"I don't know. I guess he took in the call. Hold on," he said and spoke into the phone, "Get me Frank."

They were faced away from me, so I didn't wait. I was out of sight and getting farther away from them. I turned at the corner and kept on. At the next intersection, I saw headlights approach. It was a big stake body truck, traveling at well below the posted limit. I let it roll past, jumped on its back and hauled myself up, climbing its gate slats like a ladder and over into the bed. The driver hadn't seen. Solid plate steel protected the cab's rear window. There were maybe a dozen sheets of particle board taking up most of the bed. I lay across them as the driver turned in the direction I had come. I didn't like going past those guys, but any direction should take me away from trouble. It was raining harder, now.

The two cops were in the roadway as we passed. I stayed low, but one saw me through the slats and hollered, "He's in the truck."

I watched through the tailgate as they chased but fell behind. The guy in the trench coat knelt and took aim for a couple seconds but raised his pistol skyward as we pulled farther away, out of range. The truck driver, oblivious, maintained his speed.

The Chrysler came around the corner, its flattened tire thudding on the roadway, and picked them up. I willed the truck driver to step on it. He didn't. I could hear the Chrysler's engine straining to overcome the drag of the flat. After a block, the tire shredded, and the car grew a rooster-tail of sparks as its bare rim sang along the roadway. The driver pushed it to try and keep up but nearly lost control of the big car. The truck pulled away, until the Chrysler faded in the distance and was out of sight.

We joined a chain of cars headed off the island. That was fine with me. It wasn't likely the cops could organize a roadblock, tonight. I could hop out somewhere on the Atlantic City side of the bridge and either go to ground or try to get home. A few blocks along, though, the driver turned onto a side street. I let him go a couple blocks, until it was clear he was staying in town.

I banged on the truck cab's roof. The driver, surprised, stood on the brakes and slewed to a stop. He got out and shouted, "Get the fuck off my truck." He was a little guy and wore a Fu Manchu that grew down his chin and disappeared under his lumpy jaw. He sounded drunk.

I said, "I've got cash here," I held up the bag, "I'll pay you to take me over the bridge."

"No. Get off." He squirted tobacco juice onto the wet roadway without looking away.

The rain whipped my face. I said, "Name your price."

He reached into the cab and produced a big revolver. "One. Two—"

"Okay." I didn't know what his top number would be. "Okay, I'm going." I hopped over the side, and he pulled away, tires spinning out on the wet asphalt.

I trotted down a cross street, parallel to the main drag. My car was too far away to try for, now, at least while those cops were looking for me. There would likely be more, soon. I needed wheels. I didn't have the right tools to either boost or jack another car, so I'd have to talk my way into a ride.

A few cars were traveling toward the main street. I tried to flag them down, but they passed and turned in the direction of the bridge. The rain was steady, pushed about by the wind.

Another car approached, driving toward the intersection. I reached into the bag, pulled the money from the manilla envelope and waved the bills over my head. The man driving slowed to a stop and thumbed the passenger window down a few inches. "What's going on, fella?"

"I need to get over the bridge. I'll make it worth your while."

The passenger door unlocked with a *click*. "Put your money away. Least I can do."

I got in. "Thanks."

"I were you, I'd think about getting far away." He motioned toward his car radio. It was on but too low to really hear anything.

"They upgraded the storm a little while ago. Talking about a surge."

I said, "Yeah, if I catch my friend, we'll both get out of here."

"Where you headed?"

"Philadelphia." I took off the ballcap and stuffed it in with my tools.

"I'm going to Cherry Hill, if you want to ride with me."

"That would be great. Thanks."

"Don't sweat it." He held his hand over the defrost vent. "If you can't do something nice for someone once in a while, what good are you?"

The wipers were barely keeping up with the rain. We turned onto the main drag, fell in with traffic heading out of town and traveled slowly, seven or eight blocks. An Acme Market came into sight, and traffic slowed even more, to a crawl. The driver said, "I don't understand the hold up," and took a pack of cigarettes from his shirt pocket.

Flashlights swept the area ahead. Two cops wearing dark windbreakers emblazoned with Police in bright yellow letters were stopping vehicles and speaking to the drivers. I asked, "Is that normal?"

The driver shook loose a cigarette from the pack and took it in his lips. "Never seen it. Maybe giving us a warning about what's ahead. Once we're past there, it's a long run to the bridge with nowhere to turn off." He pushed in the lighter on the dash. "Might be an accident on the causeway."

I didn't like it. We were about ten cars away when I saw the cop on the right side of a car tap on its window and speak to the passenger. They weren't giving anyone a warning. I made a show of patting my pockets and said, "Shit, I left my phone back at the job. I'll have to go back."

"That's a shame," the driver said, "Look, I'm sorry, I gotta get going."

"That's okay. Thanks, anyway." As I opened the door, the dome light popped on. I got out and shut the door but not before one of the cops noticed and motioned to his partner.

It felt like it was raining still harder. I moved quickly to the far side of the supermarket parking lot and took off running along the pavement, onto a side street and zig-zagged through the blocks, not looking back to see if they'd followed. Papers and other small debris flew by on the wind. Some places the water was deep enough to splash.

CHAPTER THREE

Only one house on the street showed light. Most were boarded up. I picked out one in the next block that wasn't shuttered but still looked empty and walked around back. Its little yard was enclosed by four foot chain-link. There was a wooden outdoor shower stall sat on the corner of a small concrete patio. The house sat on concrete footers that created an eighteen-inch-high crawlspace underneath. I had to reach over my head to touch the windowsills. The lock on the back door looked tough.

I took out my prybar, hooked the backpack on the fence where it met the house, and clambered up it, until I stood on the top rail and balanced there, leaning one hand on the wall. The wind threatened to blow me off the fence. I could reach the corner window and fit the bar's blade end between the sash and the sill, and levered it up, breaking the latch. I yanked open the sash, dropped the tool inside, lifted my bag and pushed that in too, and slid through the window headfirst, landing on the kitchen floor. I rested there for a few moments, then stood and shut the window.

My eyes adjusted. Typed lists of phone numbers and Dos and Don'ts were slid inside plastic document protectors and fixed to the refrigerator with magnets. This was an empty summer rental. The home was fitted with Ikea cabinets and Sears appliances. I tried the tap. The water was still on and the clock on the stove read 7:14, so the power, too. Probably, the house was still leased.

The living and dining room furniture was also mostly Ikea stuff. It looked like that was where they bought the pictures hung on the walls, too. I found clean towels in a linen closet and used two to dry my face and hair and blot my wet clothes. There was an access panel to the attic space in the closet ceiling.

I reasoned I'd be able to ride out the storm here and if I could, make my way back to my car as things calmed. There was nothing to eat in the refrigerator or cupboards. I hadn't expected anything, but I hadn't eaten since noon, and I'd be hungry by the time I left. I'd work that out. I took a hard plastic tumbler from a cabinet and got a drink of water from the tap. It helped. I went through the house, looking for something useful. There wasn't.

I sat at the table and opened the Manilla envelope I'd taken from Picozzi's, the one taped to the back of the painting I'd liked. Inside the envelope were three thousand dollars in crisp hundreds. Along with the money, was a pair of New Jersey driver's licenses and passports, as well as two credit cards. It was too dark in the house to make out what was printed on them. I fished around in my tool bag and found the Bic lighter I kept there and took a chance on some light.

One license showed Picozzi's face but bore another name, Albert LaBella. He knew enough to prepare for trouble but didn't know enough not to pick a name with the same number of syllables. The other license was for a Maria Chavez. I assumed that name was also an alias. Pictured on the card was a woman who appeared to be in her fifties. Both licenses showed addresses in another town.

The names on the passports matched the driver's licenses. The credit cards were a Visa and Mastercard, both in the LaBella name. There was also a single sheet of printer paper. I unfolded it. There were fourteen lines, each with a series of numbers printed out. They looked like account and routing numbers.

Picozzi had put all this together in case he needed to leave in a hurry. It was stashed close to his garage. It implied that Picozzi was into more than just straight county business. Maybe the woman was bent, too. It made me think it had something to do with my current problems. I put it all back in the envelope.

I was tired but too keyed-up to rest. Too wary, as well. I'd rest once I was away from here. I stayed back, away from the windows but kept watch, slowly moving back and forth through the house. The houses on either side were set too close to see much through those windows but the bay in front gave me a view of the street in both directions and I had fair visibility in the back of the dwelling.

I wondered again about the response for a simple house alarm. Six cops, four of them plain clothes state troopers, were more than unusual. If Picozzi was so important he rated that kind of coverage, why wouldn't Buddy know who he was? There was definitely something fucked up about that. That, and them shooting at a burglary suspect. Not just the new guy, the older guy had taken aim, later, when I was in the back of the truck. I think that was at least against any police agency's protocol. Probably broke a few laws, too. I wondered too about the roadblock. It seemed to have been organized extraordinarily quickly, especially for a small beach town readying for a storm.

The young cop I'd hurt bothered me. I'd needed to shut him up, but he'd hit his head on the pavement harder than I'd wanted. I'd also used bad judgement. In the moment, I hadn't wanted to lose time looking for his gun in the grass but now I wished I had.

I thought about Susan, too. Before I'd left, she'd said, "I'll be busy tonight." From her delivery, I'd taken that to mean *Don't call me.* It didn't matter. I couldn't call anyone. My phone was in my car and there was no landline in the house.

I'd been watching for about five minutes when I saw a police car plow through the shallow water in the street and pull to a stop at the corner, about six-hundred feet away. A few moments later, a woman struggling to hold onto an umbrella, came out of the house I'd seen lit up and went to the car. She spoke to the cop and pointed in my direction. Her umbrella blew inside-out as he turned on the car's spotlight.

I was standing just beyond the beam as it swept across the raindrops on the windowpane. I crawled to the table and pulled the backpack, letting it drop. It was heavy. For a moment, I considered hiding it all in the attic but gave it up. I didn't have time and might need the tools later. Plus, even if there were only three-thousand dollars, I'd had bad luck when I'd taken my eyes off the money. I crawled across the floor, exited through a window on the far side of the house and moved quickly through the sodden backyards, staying low, barely clearing fences, to the end of the block. Out of sight, I ran, splashing through puddling water.

CHAPTER FOUR

I ran down a side street, near the main drag, and saw a commotion on the far corner of the intersection. Four teenagers were coming out of a package store, through its broken glass door, ducking under the waist-high push bar, their arms full of liquor bottles. A short, fat kid, wearing flip flops and baggy shorts that ended mid-calf, dropped one and jumped away as it shattered on the pavement. The bunch of them whooped and laughed as they piled into a silver Impala and drove away.

Finding refuge inside an empty house still seemed a good idea. Most of the properties on the island looked to have been built post-war or newer, and most were big—three-story, three or four-unit rentals—directly fronting the sidewalks, with narrow alleys between each and almost no setback in the rear. Owners and renters here alike had little use for yard space.

I picked out one, found that its back door wasn't deadbolted, slipped the knob latch with a card and entered the first-floor apartment kitchen. I'd picked badly. There was leftover pizza and beer in the refrigerator and a couple's clothes in the bedroom. I was about to leave when I noticed a spent Jersey Lottery ticket in the bathroom wastebasket. There was a chance these people were across the inlet at one of the casinos. If so, they might decide to stay in its hotel. I'd have to keep alert but any time off the street and out of the weather was good time.

Nearby houses blocked most of the view, front and back. The front door was deadbolted. I locked the knob, too, and wedged a kitchen chair's back under the backdoor knob. These could give me another couple seconds if I missed the occupant's approach.

After that, I took a slice of cold pizza from the box and ate while I looked to see what else these people had left in the apartment. There was two hundred and fifty-five dollars rolled up in a sock in a top bureau drawer. I put it in my pocket and kept looking, A pistol would have been helpful, but I came up blank. It seemed they'd taken any other cash they had with them, too.

There was a landline. If I could get in touch with Buddy, he might be able to get me off the island or at least know somewhere I could go to ground, if I had to leave this house. I punched up his number and let it ring ten times before I hung up. There was no message. Buddy wouldn't recognize the number and figure it for spam, but if I called twice, he might think it was something important. I let it ring another ten and gave up.

I paced through the house, checking front and back at intervals but couldn't see much. I was tired from all the running I'd done. I pulled another kitchen chair from under the table and sat.

I might have dozed because I never heard a car door shut, only a couple laughing and keying the front door lock. I grabbed the chair propped against the back door and yanked it free just as the front door was opening. I cursed to myself as I ducked under the kitchen table and shifted the chairs into place as quietly as I could.

The lights came on in the living room and the guy said, "I'm getting a beer. Want one?"

"Sure. I want to get into something comfortable." I heard the woman kick off her shoes and the bathroom door close.

The guy left the lights off as he came into the kitchen but enough spilled from the front for me to see he was wearing yellow slacks and tan loafers with little tassels. Tan argyle socks, too. He opened the refrigerator and took two bottles off the shelf. I heard a cabinet door open and close, and he walked back into the living room.

The television came on as I heard the toilet flush and the door open. The woman said, "What's it saying about the storm?"

"I haven't found the news yet. The stations here aren't—here we go."

They watched and listened to the reports. I could only make out snippets of what the announcer was saying. My knees were starting to cramp. Finally, the woman said, "I think we should have stayed at the casino. This sounds bad." She was quiet for a few moments and said, "Should we go back to the casino?"

"The news people always make it sound bad. They sensationalize everything, to keep you tuned in."

"God you're cynical."

"I'm a realist."

"It looks worse than when we were driving." The guy didn't say anything. She tried again. "It looks bad out there."

"It looks like a storm." The television went silent. "I'll tell you what looks good."

She giggled. "Stop it, monorail mind. This is no time for that."

"I beg to differ. This is the perfect time."

There were quiet sounds of bodies moving on the couch and more giggling, until the woman said, "Come on, then."

They moved to the bedroom but left the door open. I heard clothes drop and the mattress squeak as they began to fool around. When I heard random moans and a rhythmic thumping sound, I crawled from under the table and went out the back door.

CHAPTER FIVE

It was a long way to where I'd left my car, and there would be police activity—I'd parked only a few blocks from Picozzi's.

Some streets were flooded up to the crown. The few cars moving plowed through the water at fairly low speed. I mostly walked across lawns, close to the house fronts. Water sloshed in my shoes. A few times I stepped into shadows or around the corner of a house as I saw vehicles approach and waited there until they passed.

Through the gaps between houses, I saw an ambulance stopped on the next street over, its lightbar flashing. In a town this size, hospital cases probably went to Atlantic City. The cops might still be checking cars heading over the bridge, but it was likely they'd wave an ambulance through.

As I cut through yards, I heard its engine drop out of hi-idle, as the driver shifted into gear. It pulled away. I yelled, "*Wait,*" and splashed into the street behind it, waving my arm but the driver didn't slow and turned off at the corner.

Behind me, someone yelled, "*Hey.*" It was a cop, leaning his head out the window of his darkened patrol wagon.

I was startled but walked toward him, waved, and stopped six feet shy of his door and said, "Hey, I'm glad you're here." I recognized him. He was the first cop who'd pulled up at Picozzi's. He'd stayed back, to hold the scene, while the others chased, so I knew he hadn't gotten a look at me.

He looked tired and said, "Everything okay?" in a tone of voice that suggested he hoped that it was but knew that likely it wasn't.

"No. I was hoping to catch them. I'm not doing well, I've got this pain in my chest, right here," I tapped myself on the sternum and said, "I gotta get to a hospital."

He sat there staring at me long enough that I readied to launch myself at his door if he tried to get out of the car—I might be able to break his arm or ankle, but he only said, "Hop in."

I walked around the front of the car and took off the backpack, laid it in the footwell and got into the passenger seat. He said, "Just gimme a minute," and busied himself, writing with a stylus on the screen of a monitor secured to the console. Without looking up, he said, "What's in the bag?"

"My hand tools. I was working, closing a place up and all the sudden felt real bad. I sat down for a while, waiting for it to go away but it didn't." He gave no sign of hearing me. I said, "Can we get going?"

"Sure, sure." He kept writing, said, "You probably pulled something. That can really hurt," slid the stylus into its slot in the laptop and looked at me. "Hand tools?"

"Yeah."

"Mind showing me?"

"Of course not." Maybe the cops who'd chased me got a better look than I'd thought and put the word out I was carrying a backpack, but I didn't think so. I'm not a scary-looking guy. In fact, I've a regular appearance, but there'd been trouble tonight. I smiled as innocently as I could and said again, "Of course not. Here." I saw now that he wasn't tired at all. Maybe only jaded. "I apologize. I should have offered to show you these before I got into your car." I hoisted the backpack to my lap and held it open.

"Oh, that's okay." He reached inside, fingering my hatchet. "I wouldn't want you to get them wet," he picked up my pry bar and said, "you know, have them get all rusty on you. Good idea, here, wrapping this with friction tape." He'd made a statement but stared at me while he held on to the bar. He wanted me to respond.

I humored him. "Yeah, easier to get a grip."

He nodded. As he put it back in the bag he said, "I'll bet it keeps them quieter while you're carrying them, too. No clanging around in your knapsack. Like—"

"I suppose so." I interrupted him and lowered the tools to the floor. "Never thought about it—"

He cut me off. "I was gonna say, while you were running," he paused, staring at me, pointed ahead, and said, "chasing after the medics. You were doing pretty good for a guy with chest pains."

"Look, if you aren't going to take me to the hospital, at least call someone who will," I leaned forward to read his nametag and said, "Officer Nolan." I put my hand on the wrecking bar. "What do you say?" If need be, I'd lay him out and take it from there.

He nodded and started the engine, turned on his headlights and pulled away. "Don't worry. I'll get you there." He drove straight through the intersection, sticking to the smaller street. "You must have left the rest of your tools on the job."

"Yeah. Can't do without these, though."

"No, I guess not." He was quiet a moment and said, "How'd you get stuck down here?"

"That's a long story."

"That's all right. We've got a long ride," he slowed at a stop sign, looked, and said, "before we get you to the hospital."

"The short version is a guy dropped me off on the job and didn't come back."

"Well, that wasn't such a long story, was it?" I let him be pleased with himself. He said, "Where is this job?"

I gestured over my shoulder with my thumb and improvised. "Over that way, somewhere. I don't know the address. Like I said, I rode down here with another guy. He dropped me off and went to take care of something in another town, but he was supposed to be back hours ago, so I don't think he's coming back."

"You didn't call him?"

"Left my phone in his truck." To stay ahead of another question, I said, "My phone and my wallet."

He opened the console. "That's rough. Here," he fished out a cell phone and said, "use mine."

"Thanks." I made no move to take it. "I've got his number saved in my phone. I couldn't tell you what it is if my life depended on it."

He chuckled and put the phone away. "That's what we do now, don't we?" He turned onto a wider street. "Cell phones will be the ruination of us all. I'll stop by the station, see if the medics are there. Maybe we can look up your buddy's number while they check you out."

"I'd rather go right to the hospital."

"This way somebody's looking at you sooner."

"Sure." He had no intention of leaving the island. "That would be great."

His radio crackled and a voice came over. I could barely understand the message. It sounded like someone was asking for a location. The cop took up his radio handset, identified his car and said, "Right now, I'm coming in with a fellow who's having some trouble." He hung it on its peg on the dash. "What's your name?"

"Wally." It was the first name that came to mind. "Wally Renninger. How about you?"

He ignored that and said, "Where you from, Wally?"

"Souderton." I didn't know how I came up with that but said, "Souderton, PA."

"That's a haul."

"Yup."

We slowed as we approached a building with a sign on its front lawn that read "Police." It looked as though two brick buildings had been pushed together to make one. Half was the municipal building and police station, with big, floor to header windows flanking the glass door and a low-pitched roof covered with fiberglass shingles. The other half of the building was the fire station. Its roof was flat, and it was fronted with large overhead doors. The truck bays were empty. In the back of the open floor was a flatbottom metal Jon boat fitted with a big outboard, all mounted on a metal trailer. I could see through the glass in the overhead doors that it was separated from the police station by an unbroken brick party wall. It seemed every light in both halves was lit but as I watched, the lights in the firehouse garage bays shut off—they must have been on a timer.

"Look at that," he said, "everybody's out, next door." The cop pulled the car into a parking spot and shut it off. "Let's see what we can do about you." He was being cute again. He said, "The girl on the desk is an EMT and I'll scare up an O2 bottle." He got out of the car and hurried to the station through the rain without looking back at me.

Chasing the ambulance blindly had been a mistake and if I weren't at a police station, I might think about dropping him. That would be a mistake, too. It might solve the immediate problem but create others. I followed him inside. I could still make something happen here.

Sat behind the counter was a young, chubby blonde-haired woman wearing a blue uniform shirt with neither sleeve patches nor badge. Her top buttons were undone, revealing a good bit of cleavage. "Hi, Jimmy." I looked at her waist. She wasn't wearing a gun belt. She said, "How long did it take Dave to get you back on the road?"

"He had us all back in service in about an hour, once he got there. Even the staties." To me, he said, "A clever fella flattened a bunch of our tires."

"Why'd you wait for him?" the woman said, "Why didn't you just change it yourself?"

"This weather? Fuck that."

"What's it like out there, now?"

"Worse." Across a hallway that paralleled the party wall with the firehouse, was a steel door to a public restroom. "This is Wally. His buddy left him here in town with no way home."

The woman said, "That sucks."

I spoke up. "I need to get to a hospital. I need medical attention. Officer Nolan, here, doesn't seem to be in any hurry."

He patted the air at me. "Whoa, easy, Wally." He wore a black rubber wedding band on his ring finger. He turned to the woman and said, "Mona, would you check him out while I see about finding some O2?"

She came out from behind the counter. "What's the trouble?"

I tapped my chest. "I'm getting sharp pains, right here."

"Oh." She sounded worried. "Here, have a seat." To the cop, she said, "Jesus Christ, Jimmy. Grab a stethoscope and BP cuff, too, please."

He said, "Uh-huh," walked away, and turned down the hall.

She shouted, "You should have taken him to the hospital." He didn't answer.

She put a hand to the side of her mouth, said, "He can be a real asshole," and winked. She looked in the direction of the bathroom. "I'm surprised he even showed up for work. He usually takes off any time there's a storm." She looked at me. "I'm Mona."

"Wally."

She took my wrist between her fingers and looked at her watch. "Most of us are a little on edge, here. On top of the storm and all, one of our guys was assaulted tonight."

"I'm so sorry. How badly?"

"Bad enough. Head injury. They wanted to chopper him to the University of Pennsylvania, there, in Philly but the birds can't go up in this soup. They have the head trauma unit there. He's over at Atlantic City."

"That's awful."

"The latest word we got is, he's doing better, now."

"Who tuned him up?"

"No telling, the guy got away. There's always a few assholes who come out whenever there's a bad storm. They take advantage of the confusion, you know? We'll get him. We always have some extra guys working overtime on nights like this, and the chief started calling in the rest of the off-duty guys once that guy was assaulted." She lowered my wrist and said, "Your pulse is a little fast but that's understandable—you're anxious. It doesn't feel like your pressure's up. I'll check it, anyway," She raised her voice to be heard by the cop, "Once I have a BP cuff and stethoscope." She listened for a response. When none came, she leaned forward and spoke more quietly. "Thing is, this guy that's hurt, he's an asshole, too, but his father's a big shot, so it's a bigger problem than it should be."

I wanted to hear more and said, "Oh, yeah?"

She didn't need much prompting. "He just got hired full time. His father got him jumped past a lot of people on the list, me included. This had only been his first summer. Real know-it-all."

I smiled at her, said, "That's disappointing," and thought about that. It answered some questions but asked a few more. As casually as I could, I slipped on my backpack. To sound friendly, I said, "Where do you sit on the list, now?"

"Two. They could still get to me."

"Good luck."

"Thanks."

Before I could ask anything, she said, "I'm pretty sure they're all out, next door."

"Yeah, it looked that way."

"I can put it out over the medic band, anyway." She put both hands behind her head and did something with her hair and arched her torso, pushing out her breasts. "Somebody will swing by."

"That would be great."

The phone rang and she went around the counter to answer it. "Police. What's your emergency?" She typed one-handed while she listened and said, "Everybody's out now, but as soon as a car's available I'll send them. Okay? All right, now." She hung up and continued to type with both hands. In the lower corner of the monitor, the time read 8:17.

I said, "So, you're 911?"

She smiled without looking up from the keyboard. "That's me."

"I'm curious, there was a break-in at—is it County Commissioner Picozzi's house?"

"County Executive." She finished and looked up. "Yeah, somebody broke in."

"How'd you get that? Alarm system?"

Her face changed. She looked puzzled but said, "No, that was a phone call. A neighbor saw the guy. Why?"

"Just curious." I wanted to keep her talking. If I found out more about Picozzi, I might find out why it all went bad. "What's the deal with Picozzi? He a rich guy?" Knowing why might help me.

She nodded. "His house is beachfront property. I've seen it, it's nice." She paused but said, "He's held that job forever cause he does well for the county, but a lot of people say he's crooked. He's supposed to have a lot of money hidden in his house. Like maybe a million."

I doubted that but smiled and said, "What do you think?"

"Oh, I don't know. It's just something I hear sometimes when his name comes up. Which really isn't a lot. He's kind of quiet, for a politician. So, who knows?" She smiled again. I got the feeling she liked me.

I heard a toilet flush and looked. The cop came out of the bathroom, speaking into his phone. "Yeah. Yeah." He looked up at me and said, "Okay then. We'll be here." He ended the call and said, "Well, I see you and Mona are acquainted."

I said, "That's right."

She said, "Where's the O2?"

"Yeah, I looked around, but I couldn't find a bottle."

A big black car pulled up out front. It could have been a Chrysler. Mona said, "This guy needs to go to the hospital, Jimmy." Two of the plainclothes cops who'd chased me at Picozzi's got out of the car.

I said, "I gotta take a piss," and walked past the cop, taking pains not to make physical contact.

He said, "Yeah, you go ahead. We'll be right here."

The bathroom was a one-seater. I closed the door behind me and threw the deadbolt, put my backpack on the sink and hauled myself up onto it, too, straddling the knapsack. I lifted the drop ceiling panel and as quietly as possible, slid it out of the way, and pulled down a six-foot batt of pink twelve-inch insulation that ran between metal rafter trusses. Those were supported by the brick party wall.

Jimmy the cop knocked on the door and said, "You okay in there, Wally?" I heard the station door open and voices, men speaking to Mona.

I counted on them not figuring what I was doing until after I did it. "Yeah, I'm fine." I pushed my backpack over the party wall into the void between the metal trusses, until its weight overwhelmed the ceiling panels next door and it fell through them to the firehouse floor. The sound was muffled but still loud.

Jimmy shook the door handle. "What are you doing in there?"

I grabbed the trusses and pulled myself up and over the top of the brick wall. I was making a lot of noise. Jimmy was banging on the door now and someone hollered, "See if you can find the key in the chief's office."

I could see into the empty firehouse through the hole the bag had made. When I'd pulled myself along far enough that my feet cleared the bricks, I swung, bringing down more of the ceiling. Panels and some of the metal struts clattered to the floor. I hung for a moment and then dropped.

I could hear the cops through the party wall, still beating on the bathroom door as I picked up my bag and went out the back.

CHAPTER SIX

wasn't too far from my car and ran in its direction. Once close, I slipped its key from my wallet. There were only a handful of cars parked on the street. Most of the houses were boarded up. I saw a glow in the direction of Picozzi's house, police portable lights glinting through the raindrops.

I stood in a shadow and scanned the area around my car. No one appeared to be watching it. I approached, unlocked it, slung my backpack through the open door and took off.

The windshield fogged. I wiped at it with my handkerchief, turned on the defrost fan, full blast and cracked open my window. Raindrops stung my face, and as the car warmed, I rolled the glass closed. The heat felt good. I was chilled to the bone.

I headed north, reasoning there must be another bridge or causeway to either the next island town or the mainland. The street I traveled ended at a nature center. A padlocked metal barricade blocked its entrance. There was a framed map of the center posted next to the gate, at least six feet broad. It revealed no way off the island, north. I bore to the left and roughly followed the island's bay side as best I could. A few times it looked hopeful, but I didn't find a way out of town.

A silver Impala flashed across my path, against the light. I stood on the brakes as a kid in its passenger seat, leaning out his open window, hurled an empty liquor bottle at the traffic signal. It shattered on contact, with a low-pitched *Clang!* that sounded over the storm. I heard them whooping and cheering as they sped away. I crossed the intersection in the wake they'd sent up, that crested over the sidewalk.

Atlantic City's distant casino lights shown through the rain. I was nearing the causeway I'd crossed over coming into town. There was no other way on or off the island by car. I'd put myself in a box. I should have checked on that before I agreed to do this job. I should have checked a lot of things.

I shut off my lights and slowed, about two blocks away from the causeway approach, near enough to see that there were still two cops on post. There were yellow sawhorses set across the road now, along with their cruiser.

I circled the block to backtrack. I was nearing a CVS when headlight beams from the cross street lit the intersection ahead. I pulled over. A big SUV turned onto the street and into the drugstore parking lot, fast, going all the way back. I heard metal on metal noises, loud enough to cut through the sounds of the storm. I wanted to see what was happening. Letting the Honda idle, I got out and crept through the lot.

Two men were attacking the steel door in back, one holding the handle of an old Kelly tool while another beat its adze edge between the door's frame and the block wall with a sledge. A third man had backed the vehicle ten feet from them and was unspooling heavy chain, flaking it out on the pavement, and hooked one end to the vehicle's steel bumper.

When the two had made a gap broad enough for purchase, they hooked the cable to the top of the doorframe.

I'd seen enough and went back to my car. These guys were going after the safe with controlled drugs—opiates, benzos, etc. I knew about a crew who did jobs like this. They'd go to a city, spend a day scouting, working out a schedule and map, rent a heavy SUV, a tractor-trailer, forklift, and a couple cars, all with hot credit cards. When they were ready, they'd hit five or six places in one night—drug stores, mostly, but any place with goods they could easily turn into money. Anything big, like a safe, they drove to wherever they'd left the semi, load it and go back out. They were good with alarms but sometimes they'd go commando—cut through roofs or walls, even concrete, with gasoline powered saws, pull ATMs and safes out of the buildings with a mechanized winch. Wild men. They worked mostly on the East Coast but would stretch out, too, taking care to avoid states like Florida or Texas, where the sentencing guidelines were particularly harsh.

These guys here, tonight, were likely operating the same way, and intended to hit every town along the shore. They'd been smart and professional, opportunistically counting on the storm to make things tough on the local law. They could neither have planned on the mess I'd stirred up tonight nor foreseen their trouble from its resulting increase of police presence.

This could be good for me. As I K-turned, I heard their engine rev, the steel door squeal free of the wall, and a loud clatter as it landed and was dragged along the pavement. The alarm system's screams faded in volume as I pulled away, and then stopped abruptly. So, these knew something about alarms, too.

I drove back to where I could watch the blockade at the causeway and pulled over. Again, I was aware of how tired and sore I was.

Local cops must have taken in the call without sirens. My first indication they'd responded to the CVS was the sound of gunshots, behind me, a quick flurry that settled into a steady volley. The volume of fire increased by the seconds, likely as more officers came on location. I wished I had a police radio.

The cops manning the causeway startled, but only acted to pull the sawhorses away and move their cruiser. Light bars flashed over the bridge in the near distance, and at intervals, four Atlantic County Sheriff's cars streamed into town. I ducked down as they flew past. There came the sound of more gunfire. I heard an automatic weapon speak. More cars flashed through the checkpoint but neither of the cops on post moved. The gun-fire dwindled and stopped.

I sat there, disgusted, resting for a few minutes more. The cops were dragging one of their sawhorses back, across the road when another car, a white Cadillac sedan, came slowly toward them, over the causeway. One cop put up a hand and patted the air in front of him and the Caddy stopped. He approached the driver and pointed in the direction they'd come. I assumed he was telling them to turn back. They spoke and then the cop held up his hand again and thumbed up a number on a cell phone, never taking his eyes off them. His partner stood back but watched them, too. The first cop put the phone to his ear and spoke and then, nodded, put his phone away and waved the car through.

It came in my direction. I leaned back, over the console, into the shadows but watched as they passed. There were four serious-looking men in the car. If they'd been police, they'd have simply badged their way past the barricade and onto the island. These were thugs, mercenaries. I had no doubt they were looking for me. It was about money, now.

CHAPTER SEVEN

During the evening, I'd seen lights from tall buildings across the inlet, but also from one on the island itself, somewhere north of the causeway, towering over everything else on the horizon. It was a high rise, six or seven blocks distant. Here, in a resort town like this, it had to be a hotel.

I had some identification in my wallet but nothing usable. Everything I carried was in my own name and would document my presence if I tried to use it. I'd have to take a chance with one of Picozzi's cards with the fake name. It could be a problem if they wanted to see identification. I didn't look anything like him, and he seemed to be at least thirty years older but I'd try to go with it. I couldn't know if any of the cops who'd gone inside Picozzi's house knew about or noticed his Manilla envelope of fake ID missing from its spot behind the painting but even if they did, they might not anticipate this move.

As I zig-zagged through the streets toward the high rise, I knew I'd also be taking a chance with making my face public. It was certain there'd be security cameras in the lobby and likely every hallway on every floor, too. The ballcap was all I could do to alter my appearance. At this point, though, shelter was going to be necessary. I'd need to take the chance.

This was taking a chance with my Honda, too. Likely, there were cameras in the parking lot. If I saw any trouble here, a search could link me to the car. I made a turn and water sounded against the undercarriage. If I left it parked on the street and the water rose, it could ruin the car anyway. I drove on for a few blocks and turned into the hotel garage. It was surprisingly full, and I didn't find an empty spot until the fourth level up. I backed into a spot, got my backpack, walked down the steps and into the hotel proper.

Across the lobby, I could see through glass doors that their thresholds had already been blocked with Pigs—water absorbent flood barriers, even though the entrance was a few steps up from the street.

I walked up to the clerk on the desk. "I'm hoping you can help me." On his jacket pocket was embroidered, *The Bayshore*. Fixed to the wall behind him was a large dial clock without numerals. The hours were indicated by long thin lines that spread from its center, more like a compass face than clock. It was only 8:50. It felt later. "I missed my ride home and now I'm stuck here. Is there any chance I can get a room?"

"That is unfortunate, sir." He began typing on a computer keypad. "We can certainly accommodate you." To be pleasant he looked up and said, "How is it outside, now?"

I smiled and said, "It's as bad as it looks."

He looked back at the monitor and said, "I can put you in a room on the fifth floor."

"You're a lifesaver."

Picozzi's fake card worked without a problem. The desk clerk handed me a key card and said, "Here you are Mister LaBella. There are toiletries in the room, but if you need anything else, just give us a call here at the desk."

"I will." I needed something to eat. "By any chance, is your kitchen still open?"

"Yes, it's a shortened menu, but they're still serving, or you can order from your room."

"That's great. Thank you."

"You're welcome, sir."

I took the elevator to the fifth floor and found my room. It wasn't anything special, but it was clean and dry. I put my tools on the luggage stand, took up the phone and ordered food.

I stripped off my clothes, wrung them out and rolled them in towels to make them a little less wet. I set the fan speed to high on the room's heater and draped my jacket and pants over the unit's vents. Given the chance to stop running, I tried to think. Much of the night didn't make sense but I was tired and would need more information to make things clear.

I picked up the phone, asked the girl at the desk to get me an outside line and punched up Susan's number. It rang five times, and she picked up. "Hello."

I hadn't counted on her answering and for a moment had nothing to say. She said, "Are you all right?"

"Yes."

"I see you're calling from Atlantic County. Is this the one phone call?"

"No, not at all. I just decided to stay over instead of driving home through this slop." She was quiet and I said, "I'd call a lawyer if I were in trouble."

"Right. You certainly wouldn't call me for anything important."

I hadn't known what to expect but it wasn't this. "You know that's not what I meant. I wouldn't want to make law enforcement aware of you. Of course, I'd get word to you."

"That's comforting."

She wasn't letting me start a conversation. I said, "I didn't call you to argue."

"Why did you call?"

That was a good question. "I just felt like we needed to talk."

'You might need to. I don't."

I took a breath and as calmly as I could, said, "I know that you've been unhappy with how things are with us, and I'd like to change that."

"I don't think you do. This was all supposed to be about getting out from under. You accomplished that a while ago."

"I don't work that much."

"Work." She sounded out the word. "That's rich."

"That's what it is."

"Nobody gets killed while I'm doing *my* work."

"Most of the time, nobody does when I do, either."

"*Not lately.*" She'd almost shouted. I had nothing to say to that. The past year I'd had more than my share of bad luck.

She spoke more quietly. "Can you just tell me one thing?"

I listened until I realized she was waiting for a response. "Sure. Ask me anything."

She spoke slowly, as though carefully. "We both have jobs. We can cover everything we have to and have money left over, without any of your—"

I cut her off. "You can cover things. I can't without this."

"Your job pays fine—look, I don't want to get off the subject. Let me finish."

"Then just ask me what you want to know."

She paused and said, "How much is enough?"

I hadn't anticipated that. I didn't know the answer. I said, "It's not a matter of what's enough or isn't. It's just so I can stay ahead of things." I realized how weak this sounded even as I said it.

"What does that mean?" She waited for me and said, "That's the worst part. You don't know." She sounded sad. "You don't know why you do this."

It wasn't a question. It was a statement. I never thought in terms of my own motivation.

I said, "It didn't upset you when we met."

I realized as soon as I said it that I shouldn't have. I expected her to flip and hang up, but she said, "You're right, it didn't bother me. It should have but it didn't. Any time you left, I'd convince myself I was frightened for you—for you and frightened about what you were doing but I really wasn't. I thought it was hot." She stopped speaking and I thought she was getting upset but when she spoke again, she sounded calm. "It turned me on." She paused and spoke more quietly. "It wasn't the money. Those times you'd come home from somewhere, some job, maybe you had money, maybe not. I didn't care. I'd just know. I'd check the papers from where you'd been. Sometimes I'd find something. Maybe just a tiny story, a one-inch column. You'd never talk about it, but I'd think to myself, 'I know who did that,' and it would give me chills. That's how fucked up I am."

"That doesn't make you fucked up."

"I'm being honest with myself, and I don't like who I am. Living out some sort of vicarious—I won't be that person, anymore. You've—the things you've done to people—I can't—"

A patrol car pulled up out front. "None of them were good people."

"*You're not a good person.*" It sounded like she was crying. "I think—I knew—" She was quiet for a few moments and said, "I know this is what you do but I guess I didn't accept that this is who you are." She hesitated but added, "Who I am."

Two cops got out and walked to the entrance. "I'm going to have to call you back."

As if I hadn't spoken, she said, "Tell me the truth. Have you done this all your life? Is this just who you are?"

Another car pulled into a spot out front that wasn't a parking space. I started pulling on my clothes. "I really have to get off the phone. How about I give you a ride to the airport in the morning?"

"I *knew* you were in trouble." She was crying plainly, now. "You're a liar."

I improvised. "No, Baby, I'm in the lobby. Other people are waiting to use the phone. I'll see you in the morning. Your flight's at eight-fifteen, right?"

"I've got my own way to the airport. I don't want a ride from you."

I said, "Okay, I understand. How about this: I'll meet you there to see you off?" I waited but realized I was listening to dead air—she'd ended the call. I hung up, grabbed my things and tugged on the ballcap, low, just above my eyes. As an afterthought, I took the little bottle of aftershave from the bathroom and stepped into the hallway, locking the door behind me.

There was no way to know if the cops had been alerted by Picozzi's bogus credit card that I'd used at the desk or if someone had spotted me in the lobby. Or if this police visit was coincidental or random. It didn't matter. I had to clear out.

Those cops would likely use the elevator. I went past it, into the empty stairwell and stood behind the door. If anyone was watching the security monitors, I would give them a lot to see but I didn't have another choice. I heard the elevator motor run and stop and heard its door open. I waited a few moments and opened the fire tower door a crack to look down the hallway. Two uniform cops wearing work jackets and clear plastic covers on their hats walked toward my room along with the desk clerk and a red jacketed hotel security guard. One of the cops unsnapped the button on his holster flap.

I took the stairs to ground level and peered out. Two more cops waited in the lobby. Bluff was with them, too. A badge in a plastic holder was hung around his neck

I ran back up to the second floor and tried doors without room numbers or those marked Employees Only. A door to a utility closet was unlocked and I stepped in, closing its door behind me. Inside were two plastic housekeeping carts with cleaning supplies up top and fresh linen stacked on the bottom shelves. Among the bottles of glass cleaner and disinfectant on one cart was a nearly full plastic quart bottle of hand sanitizer. There was a sprinkler head in the ceiling.

I tipped one of the carts, dumping its top tray of supplies and righted it again. It was heavy, but I managed to stack the other cart on top of the first and doused the shelves of clean towels and linen with the sanitizer. I dumped the aftershave on it, too.

The sprinkler would go off quickly and trigger the alarm but inside the cabinets, fire would burn unchecked for a while, protected from the sprinkler's discharge. The fire wouldn't go anywhere but would produce lots of smoke and that was what I needed.

I unwound a roll of paper towels and twisted a few feet of it to make a trailer and ran it from the cart to the closet doorway. With a bottle of Windex in its threshold to prop it open a few inches, I lit the trailer with my Bic and went back to the stairwell.

It took nearly a minute before the fire alarm went off. Its shrieking hurt my ears as I waited for guests to begin exiting. They came, first in a trickle and then a gout as more of them crowded the stairs.

The cops would be looking for the ballcap, now. I stuffed it in my backpack and left the stairwell, walking along between two annoyed middle-aged women and a couple in their twenties.

The lobby was already crowded, groups of people milling around trying to talk to each other over the wailing of the alarm. Two cops were in a shouted conversation with the staff. I moved toward the front doors but saw a uniform standing there. I hesitated a moment, deciding if I should try to go past him, when he stopped another, older man. I could make out the guy protesting but heard the cop say, clearly, "We want everyone to shelter in place, for the time being."

I went in the other direction, across the lobby, toward the door to the parking garage. I moved deliberately, through the center of the crowd, skirting the area near the front desk. It was most crowded, with guests shouting questions to the staff. Red lights flashed across the far wall of the lobby as a fire engine pulled to a stop outside, its siren winding down.

A red jacketed hotel security man was stationed near the exit to the parking garage. He was old, and looked like a retired cop. Focused on him, I had lost sight of Bluff and went past him and another cop in plainclothes, as I worked my way toward the door. The other cop held a hand over his cell phone and said, "He wants to know why you didn't take the scene at the CVS?" They either hadn't recognized or noticed me. I pushed through the rest of the crowd.

The security guy stood in my way and raised his voice to be heard over the alarm. "I need you to stay in the lobby, here, sir." The way he said *sir* sounded like he resented it, and his need for this job.

I kept walking. "I left my medication in the car."

He raised his hands to stop me. I hooked his throat with the crook of my arm and dragged him along as I went through the door. He felt solid enough, but I'd pulled him off balance and he couldn't get set. His strangled, *"Hey,"* went unheeded. Just inside the garage, he stumbled and fell but grabbed my ankle. I reached down, took a handful of his jacket at the hem and yanked it up, over his head. His arms were effectively trussed. Blinded and handcuffed this way, he struggled ineffectually until I slammed him face-first against the concrete garage floor, twice. He stopped moving. I dragged him between two parked cars and pushed him under one.

I was hoping that the cops would think I'd cleared out somehow. That way, I could get into my car and sit out the worst of the storm there, in the garage. It was what I should have done in the first place. When the weather calmed, I could drive away and try to get out of town.

They didn't know what I was driving or even if I had a car. Mine was four levels up from the street, backed into a space along the outside wall, about midway up the span. I took the stairs two at a time. When I saw the Honda, I made my way toward the front wall. The street adjoining the garage entrance was clotted with vehicles.

I unlocked the car and got in. From its driver's seat, I could see across the ramp. The gaps between floors described long, narrow triangles, and through them, between the cars parked opposite me, I could watch the ramps leading up and down to mine. If they drove, I'd duck below the dashboard. If they came on foot, I'd play it by ear.

In a few minutes I caught glimpses of two walking up the lower ramp. They were moving slowly, looking into every car. Both carried pistols. When they neared the turn, I started the Honda and pulled out, driving in their direction. I counted on them not hearing me over the alarm and the storm. I whipped the car around the turn and floored it as one stepped out from the side of an SUV. He looked up too late, and I caught him across the knees. He flipped across the hood and crushed the windshield with his back, landing in a heap on the ramp alongside me. I drove past him, flat out, staying low in the seat, struggling to see through the cracked glass. His partner loosed three rounds in my direction before I was around the next turn. One shattered the back window and punched through the ruined windshield. He tried again, through the gap between ramps as I flashed by but he missed, cleanly.

Two circuits later, I made the final turn and was less than a hundred feet shy of the street when a patrol car pulled across the exit from my right and stopped. The cop saw me coming. I floored the accelerator, braced and T-boned his car before he pulled away. The impact crushed the driver's side and broke both windows. The cop was moving, but slowly.

I saw movement, two men at the far end of the next block, running toward the crash. I yanked on the handle, but my door was jammed from the impact. The windows wouldn't go down, either. I pulled the headrest from the passenger seat and back-handed its post into the window, twice, without result. The third time, the tempered glass went white at impact and shattered an instant later, hundreds of tiny diamonds falling both on the pavement outside and into my lap. I rolled through the empty window frame, fell to the concrete and got to my feet. I felt rocky from the impact but still okay. A car, two blocks away was coming fast. The guys up the street began shooting at me, on the run. The shots all went wide. One round hit the Honda's fender as I snatched my bag and ran back up the ramp.

With both cars immobile at the entrance, I didn't worry about pursuit by vehicle in here. I ran across, toward the center of the structure, between two parked cars and rolled up onto the next level.

They'd get organized and try to bracket me. I couldn't hear anything over the noise of the alarm and storm and stayed low. I knew that the guy who shot at me was somewhere in the structure. I assumed there were others too, but it was impossible to get a sense of how many. It didn't matter. The longer I stalled and hid, the more reinforcements would come. I had to get out.

Looking across the deck under the parked cars, I could make out a pair of boots, pacing, at the top of the ramp. From his position, the man could survey two levels of the garage. I crawled toward him on my belly, hugging the inner barrier, once rolling behind tires as he moved into my line of sight. I heard him shouting to someone. I couldn't make out what he was saying over the noise of the alarm. I looked. He stood there, his hands on the top rail.

I got up and ran at him, hard. In that moment, the alarm stopped. He sensed movement and started to turn, but he was too late. I dropped my shoulder and hit him solidly, high enough to knock him back and over the rail as I'd hoped. He fell screaming and landed in a heap at the feet of the guy he'd been talking to. His arm was bent at an unnatural angle, but he was still making a lot of noise, so I figured he'd live.

The other guy and I looked at each other. He drew his pistol and sent two rounds at me, but I'd already gotten away from the rail. I recovered my tools and ran to the far corner of the ramp. My ears still rang from the alarm. It was about fifteen feet down to ground level. There was no one in either direction. I dropped the backpack. It splashed as I hiked myself up, over the rail, hung and dropped, rolling as I hit the ground. In a second, I was up and away, into the neighborhood.

CHAPTER EIGHT

August knocked me over. Pushing myself up, off the pavement, a distant streetlight glinted off the surface. Everything—the street, sidewalk, yards—was covered with seawater as far as I could see, as though the town had sprung up whole from a dark, swirling ocean.

Something big rolled and bounced toward me. I scrambled out of the way, falling as it tumbled past—a forty-gallon plastic trash can. It kept blowing away, end over end, as I recovered. Shelter could be a matter of survival.

It hadn't worked out for me, back there at the hotel, but I'd taken a cop and two civilians out of the chase, and that way more would be busy tending to them. I'd take what I could get but knew it was worse than I'd first thought. The details didn't matter. Neither did the numbers. These cops were in recovery mode. They didn't need to fabricate a rationale for enlisting every straight cop on the island, either. McCarthy, the young cop I'd put in the hospital did that for them.

I needed to arm myself and thought about Picozzi's little pistol. Odds were, it was still in the toilet tank, where I'd dropped it. I worked my way through the neighborhood toward his house, along a thin stretch—a setback—just inside the dunes, stumbling, fighting the wind. Twice, between houses, I saw patrol cars, cruising. Where a street leading to the beach dead-ended, windblown seawater streamed inland through a beach walkway. I turned down that street and kept on, sticking to alleys and backyards as much as possible. Many places, water covered the tops of my shoes and up to my ankles. From what I could see of the streets, there weren't many cars on the road. I had to fight my way through the wind. I wasn't sure what I was looking for. I needed to get inside somewhere, though. Another gust that nearly knocked me over, peeled a broad swath of roofing from a nearby three-story twin. Its shingles took off like a deck of cards.

I saw a light in the next block. I was coming up to a row of businesses on the main drag. The light came from its back. Through the plate glass in front, I saw some movement.

I ran across the street, around the block and approached as stealthily as possible. When close enough, I saw a man, wheeling boxes of goods out the back door with a hand truck and loading them into the back of a van. Likely, he was nervous about the coming surge and wanted to get vulnerable items to higher ground. It could be a way for me out of town.

Once he'd swung the hand truck around and back into the store, I moved quickly and looked into the back of the van. There wasn't enough stock to conceal myself behind.

I stepped through the store's back door. Loose packing peanuts floated in the dirty seawater on the floor. The room contained a small furnace and water heater, a breaker box and alarm keypad on the wall and water meter on the incoming service near the floor. A broom and mop leaned against the side wall and a trashcan stood in the corner. The opposite side of the small room was bare, I supposed empty of stock now in the van.

I heard the slosh of the hand truck wheels rolling through the water and pushed myself between the water heater and side wall. If he looked, he'd see me, but I was counting on his preoccupation and rush to give him tunnel vision.

It did. He made four more trips, I assumed with the most expensive things in the store. I considered going back outside and hiding in the van, or even asking him for a ride but rejected both ideas. If he found me hiding it could get weird. If I asked and he turned me down, I would have to hurt him or would still be out on the street, looking.

Red lights flashed through the open back door onto the wall, and I heard a car pull up and stop, and a man call out, "Hey. What's going on?"

"Hi, officer. I was gonna leave this but now I got to get as much stuff as I can out of the store and off the island. The forecasts are calling for a surge."

"Hurry it up. That van's liable to blow over if it gets any worse out."

"Don't worry, this is my last load."

The cop pulled away.

The guy finished and closed up, setting the alarm and locking the door from the outside. I came out from behind the water heater and let myself into the store proper. It was typical—on one side were two long glass cabinets, still filled with stock—mostly phones but other things, too. More items were mounted on the wall behind the counters—wires and cables, chargers, etc. The opposite wall was mostly shelves holding computers and monitors. The cabinets below waist level in the store had been emptied by the man with the van.

If not for the trash floating in three inches of seawater, it could almost look like it was ready for business. I looked for a store phone, but there wasn't one. A couple cheap, pay as you go phones were hung on the wall behind the counters. I cut one out of its packaging and plugged its charger into the receptacle behind the card scanner.

I wanted to know more about Picozzi. There was a guy in Philadelphia named Harry who I did business with sometimes. Harry was probably near Picozzi's age, and he knew a lot of people and things.

A tone sounded and the phone's screen lit up. There was a dial tone and I punched up Harry's number. It went to message.

I killed the call and dialed the number again. After it rang a few times, Harry answered. "Who is this?"

"The last time I saw you, you told me I should call before I came to your house."

The noise from the storm fed back and sounded over the phone's speaker. Harry was quiet for a moment and said, "By the area code I'm seeing, it doesn't look like you'll be coming by anytime soon."

"No."

"In fact, it looks like you're in a bad place to be, right now."

"I've been in better. How are you doing?"

"My arthritis is bothering me. It's the weather. What can I do for you?"

"What do you know about a guy named Charlie Picozzi?"

"From Atlantic County? That Charlie Picozzi?"

"Yeah."

"Why?"

"I want to know what he can do if he's annoyed."

"I only heard one story about him and that was from a long time ago. He got his start with Frank Farley. Hap—Hap Farley. You know anything about that guy?"

"Only that they named a rest stop for him."

"Well, Hap Farley's the man that brought gambling to Atlantic City. Other people helped it along, but Hap was the guy that got it done."

I thought about the photo in Picozzi's office. So, that's who Hap was. I said, "In that case, a place to gas up and empty your bladder seems an ignominious tribute."

"Maybe." Harry was quiet for a few moments. "Maybe not. Not much of the money ever went where it was supposed to. Besides the casinos and strip clubs, Atlantic City is still just a slum with a beach."

"What's the story you heard about Picozzi?"

"Right, right, Picozzi. Sometime around Sixty-nine, Seventy, Philadelphia Magazine did a cover story on Farley. Hap wasn't happy. He liked low visibility. The magazine couldn't even scare up a photograph of the man. They put a cartoon picture of him on the cover, a caricature, you know?

"A reporter from the magazine called him, asked for an interview. Farley's pissed—he figured they wouldn't have anything good to say no matter what he told them. He hangs up and calls in his crew. None of them have any good ideas, they're arguing. Picozzi's this young guy, maybe twenty. New. He says, 'Shut up. Here's what we're gonna do.'"

I said, "I like this guy."

"Don't interrupt me. I'll lose the thread. What he did, he put together an army of guys in vans and the morning the magazine hit the street, they bought up the entire run. He got a list from the distributor of every store, newsstand, any place that sold it, anywhere. He covered the whole Tri-State area. The only people who read the story were people with subscriptions, and that wasn't many. After that, he was Farley's golden boy.

"Anyway, you wanted to know what he can do if he's annoyed, that ought to give you an idea. What did you do to piss him off?"

"That's not important. Do you know how he made his wad?"

"What wad? What are you talking about?"

"He's a degenerate gambler. Pisses away twenty grand every weekend."

"I doubt it. That's more than a million dollars a year."

"Some people do."

"Not people who are County Commissioners."

"They're called County Executives, now."

"County Executives don't have that much money to lose, either. Where did you hear this?"

"It doesn't matter." I thought a moment and said, "Do you a guy down here named Buddy?"

"Buddy who?"

"I never heard. Deals cards. Also does the same kind of things you do."

"Tall, skinny guy? Broken nose?"

"Yeah. What do you know about him?"

"I met him once. We never did any business, but I heard he's reliable. Tough. Came up in Ducktown, there, in the city. Same as Picozzi. What do you need to know?"

"Anything else you know about him."

"Not much. Like I said, I never had any business with the guy. He's been doing this a while, so he must know how to count at the end of the day. I also heard he has connections overseas that can turn hot dollars into safe, but I can't swear to that."

"Ever hear about him getting chatty?"

"With cops?"

"Yeah."

"I never heard that, but we all roll around in the same mud. I can ask around if you want, but it'll take a while."

"No, don't bother." Through the display window, I watched as a patrol car slowed to a stop out front. I kept still and said, "You know, this is a safe phone, but I think we've talked enough." If the cop got out, I'd have to back-door him, and try to lose him in the neighborhood. "Thanks for your help."

"You're welcome. Come by sometime. Call first." He hung up.

The police car sat another few seconds and pulled away. I supposed it was the cop who'd spoken with the owner, checking to see that he'd left. I turned over a waste basket and sat behind the counter. What Harry had said bothered me, but I needed to concentrate on the present. I couldn't know if the owner was coming back but I doubted it. I figured on riding out the storm here and trying for a way off the island when it let up.

That idea lasted until the wind uprooted a street sign and flung it through the store's display window. The alarm shrieked and strobes flashed before the last shard of plate glass hit the floor. I went out the back.

CHAPTER NINE

I broke the pane nearest the doorknob, reached through and unlocked it. The door led from the back patio to the kitchen. The homeowner had prepared for the storm by shutting down the utilities. The refrigerator was empty, its door propped open with a kitchen chair. The power was off and when I tried it, no water came from the tap. I tried the stove, too, with no result. There were a few sundries in the cabinets—teabags, a box of Bisquick—but not much else.

I looked around. This was a cop's house. There were some framed photos and citations hung on the walls, along with the typical family pictures. Reading one, it was apparent that the man had worked in Philadelphia and was likely retired. The action he'd been cited for had happened in the eighties. On the wall near the stairs to the second floor was his badge, framed under glass. It might help. I took it off the wall, broke the glass against the banister post, pulled free the badge and fastened it inside my wallet.

Fixed in the closet floor of the front bedroom was a small safe. I went to work on it and had it open in about twenty minutes but found it empty. I'd been hoping there was a weapon. The guy had likely emptied the safe before he'd left.

There wasn't anything else here for me but at least it was four walls and a roof. I could ride out the worst of the storm and find a way off the island later—tomorrow night, if I needed to wait that long. I sat in a living room chair that afforded me a view of the street.

I must have been more tired than I realized. I'd dozed off and came awake with a start. I wasn't sure why until I heard a *thump* from somewhere outside. I slid down off the chair and crawled to the side window.

Outside, a silver Impala was idling in front of the house next door, its driver behind the wheel. At least two people were standing on the side of the house, near me. One, a fat kid, wearing baggy shorts that ended mid-calf, stood tiptoe and tried to look through the frontmost side window. The other was reaching to push up on the sash on the next. This was the bunch I'd seen earlier, looting the liquor store. I heard another hard thump. A fourth must be trying to force the back door.

I wanted their car. I could probably go out and take the driver, while the others were busy, but it might be better to thin their numbers, first. One looked toward my direction. I moved to the kitchen.

I needed a non-lethal weapon. My hand tools were either too heavy—like my prybar or hatchet—or too light to be effective. The kitchen table was old. Its top was scuffed white Formica. It stood on rusting, chromed steel legs that screwed into brackets on its underside. I undid one that stood against the wall. It was about three feet long, and lighter than I'd have liked but would work. I unlocked the back door and waited in the near corner of the dining room.

I heard them come up on the porch and rattle the front doorknob. One said, "Fuck this. Let's go home and smoke weed."

Another said, "Try the back." I noticed I'd left my backpack on the dining room table, but it shouldn't matter.

The pressure in the house changed as they opened the back door. One laughed, saying, "Fucking idiots. Let's see what they got." I heard the cabinet door open.

The first said, "The TV's a piece of shit," came into the dining room without looking either way and walked past me into the living room.

A kid breeched the doorway and was saying, "I'll check upstairs—" as I swung the table leg into his face. He fell and I caught the first kid across the ear as he was turning. The fat kid was faster than I'd thought and tackled me, knocking us both into the dining room table. It pitched over, onto its side, spilling my tools. I lost the table leg, and it rolled across the floor, away from me. The first had gotten to his feet. The fat kid had me in a bear hug, trying to squeeze me into submission while he bathed me in his booze-breath. I hooked him twice, on the ear, grabbed his balls and twisted, hard, breaking his grip. He screamed, rolled away and vomited all over his shirtfront, gagging. The other swung a kick at my head that I dodged. The third kid was at the door, scrabbling at the locks. I groped for the tools strewn across the carpet, came up with my awl and drove it through the top of the second kid's foot and into the floor. He dropped, screaming. I scrambled to my feet, but the third kid had bolted, yelling something to the driver.

I heard the Impala rev and its tires spinning out on the flooded roadway. I gathered up my tools, cursing. The two on the floor were moaning but would live. Even with the door wide open I could smell the fat kid's puke. The other kid screamed as I tread on his foot and wrenched my awl free. I wiped its shaft on the arm of the sofa, stepped out into the rain and moved away. I needed something else.

CHAPTER TEN

Four pale rectangles fought to show themselves in the distance, barely contrasting with the black sky. As I neared, they proved to be a row of unfinished homes, covered with white Tyvek, torn in places, flapping in the wind. The builders had boarded over its door and window openings. If I could get inside without attracting attention, I might be okay for the night.

I went between two houses and stumbled over something in the set-back, lengths of half inch copper tubing, laid there in a rough stack. Near were a few loose coils of white-jacketed #14 wire. Against the back wall of most, a particle board sheet meant to cover a ground-floor window was propped against the wall under its opening. One lay nearby, half under flood water.

Sounds came from the end house. I hiked myself up and over the wet sill. Inside, the structure seemed to breathe, flexing as the wind direction shifted, alternately pushing and pulling through the empty window frame. I glanced around. Plywood subfloor was in place throughout—here and upstairs, but the walls were unclad. Stairs had not yet been installed, either. An aluminum extension ladder raised in the open stairwell led to the second floor. Electric wiring had been roughed in—run through the walls and pulled through the blue plastic junction boxes—but there were no receptacles or switches yet. On the floor was some odd lumber and a tarp, but nothing I could use. A clattering, metallic crash sounded from what was to be the kitchen, as a length of half-inch copper tubing fell across the floor.

The storm covered the small noises I made as I climbed the ladder, and I slowly put my head through the opening and saw a man wearing a Phillies cap backwards, kneeling along a three-foot wide partition frame, opposite a bathtub, sawing its remaining water line with a narrow hacksaw. I watched him a few seconds more and said, "Hey."

He started and dropped the saw, and said, "Look, I don't want any trouble."

I ignored that while I came up the rest of the way, and said, "Wouldn't that be easier with a tubing cutter?"

He was still and quiet for a few seconds, but said, "No. I mean, yeah, I got one but there isn't enough space to run it around the pipe." He spoke haltingly, not sure what I was about or how he should play this. "The saw's better. I could take the blade out of the frame if it was real tight." A two-foot pry bar sat on the floor within his reach.

I stood where I was. "How much have you cut away, so far?"

"Just a couple lengths."

"And the pipe from the other houses." He didn't respond. I said, "You're yanking the wire, too."

"Hey, who the fuck are you, man?"

"This is who the fuck I am." I brought my wallet out and showed him the badge. "All this, the damage, stolen copper, you're looking at a third-class felony, at least."

He put his hands up and said, "Look man, just let me leave and I won't be back. Swear to god."

"Not yet." As we spoke, my eyes got used to the darkness there and I saw him more clearly. Like a lot of burglars, he was small, and thin. I said, "How were you planning to take it away?"

He took a few moments, still wondering how this was going to play, and said, "I got a van." He stole a glance at the pry bar.

"Where?"

"It's a few blocks away." He put his hands down and seemed to be readying himself.

I said, "Don't even think about it."

He leaned away from the tool and showed his hands again. "No, no, I wasn't gonna do nothing."

"Do you live on the island?"

The change up confused him, but he pointed and said, "Nah, I got a trailer in a lot, out that way, just off route nine." He shrugged. "If it hasn't floated away, yet."

"What was your plan?"

"I *was* gonna go home, but they got a roadblock set up on the causeway."

"Why not try to cross the bridge, anyway? Do the local cops know you, or are you worried about them checking your van?"

"Checking the van. They shouldn't know me. I don't come here a lot. What the fuck, man?" I suppose my questions revealed something to him. Emboldened, he said, "You ain't no cop. Why don't you go—"

"No, I'm worse." That shut him up. I said, "What are you going to do, then?"

More soberly, he said, "There's this girl I know, lives in town, here. I'll ride it out at her place, once I'm done with this here, and see what happens once the storm blows over."

Almost as if to claim that wouldn't happen soon, the wind picked up and hammered rain against the side of the house. When it slowed, I said, "What if she isn't home?"

He shook his narrow head. "She never leaves."

"What if she has?"

He might have smiled. "I got in here, didn't I?"

"What if she has company?"

He paused and said, "I'll have to—" and stopped It seemed he hadn't thought of that, or maybe didn't like the idea. "I'll see what I can talk her into."

"Is there swag in your van now?"

"No." He acted like that was a stupid question. "Not until I'm ready to go. That way, if I got surprised here, the worst they could do is get me for trespass. Once the copper is in my possession, it puts things in a whole different category."

"Smart." I gestured to take in the house. "How much will the tubing and wire from these places get you?"

"Don't know. Depends on the going price of copper." He saw that I was waiting for an answer. "Maybe three, four hundred. I don't know." Maybe worried I meant to hold him up he said, "Some places won't take this off me. They seen me around too much."

"I'll give you five hundred dollars to take me with you to this girl's house."

He'd gotten the wrong impression. "She's not—"

I put up a hand and said, "I stay in her living room."

That calmed him but he said, "Well, I don't know. She might not like it."

"You'll give her some of your money."

"How much?"

"That's for you two to work out."

"Okay." He nodded. "Okay, that could work."

"Good." Once there, I'd take everyone's phone and we'd all stay up, together.

He said, "What do I do about the copper?"

"Come back and get it. After you take me to Atlantic City in the morning."

"I don't know." He thought for a few moments. "I'll need to see it. The money, I mean. I want to see it."

I shrugged off the backpack, took out Picozzi's envelope and pulled the bills, fanning them. "Satisfied?"

"Yeah, that'll work. Okay."

He stood and made to pick up his tools. I said, "Leave them here. You can get them when you come back for the copper."

"They could walk before I get back."

"That's right."

He took a few moments and said, "Come on."

I got on the ladder first, slid the rails to the floor and moved back too quickly for him to try anything, if he'd been thinking about it. He came down, a rung at a time and said, "I'm not stupid, man."

"Good."

"My name's Lenny."

"Okay."

He waited for me to tell him mine, then shrugged and went over the sill, through the empty window frame, into the storm. I followed him, outside, and we trotted a few blocks away, through rain and wind-blown trash, to a late eighties, gray primer-painted Dodge van, parked at a curb, water to its hubs. He unlocked his door. I said, "Show me the back, first."

He came around, his shoulders hunched against the rain and said, "See for yourself, if you gotta." Inside were trash—mostly scraps of lumber and building materials—and a cracked, stained plastic milk carton full of things like motor oil and tire tools.

I made to swing a door shut but he said, "Here, if you don't do it the right way, it comes open on you." He shut the first carefully, holding the button and pushing it into place. He slammed the other, kicked its bottom edge and tested it, pulling on its handle.

I got into the passenger seat. He pulled himself up, into the driver's seat, pumped the gas pedal a few times and turned the key. It didn't catch for a few revs and then did, seeming to wheeze. Lenny held the wheel, tapping the gas to keep it running. In a few moments, the engine ran more smoothly. He shifted into gear, and we pulled into the street.

I saw no one else in either direction. Lenny drove without lights but seemed to know the streets well enough to navigate through the dark. "Her place's just a few more blocks, up this way." Water churned up by the van's tires sounded against the wheel wells.

Lenny slowed and leaned forward as a gust hammered rain against the windshield. Something about a foot square slammed into the glass in front of his face. "Fuck!" He seemed to jump back in his seat and then he laughed. "That scared the shit out of me." I was startled, too, and reminded of how anxious I felt. Lenny said, "Least it didn't crack the windshield, whatever that was," and resumed speed as the rain slowed again.

We turned onto the main street and covered a short distance when a block ahead, a stake body truck turned into the opposing lanes and washed us with its headlights.

We passed each other. Lenny sped up and watched the reflection in his side-view. "Oh, fuck me." He sounded more annoyed than worried. "Asshole."

I looked through the rear van door windows and saw the truck completing a U-turn to follow us. It was the same truck I'd jumped into, early in the evening. The van's engine ran louder but we didn't seem to be moving any faster. The truck gained quickly, its high beams bothering us both. I'd seen that guy's gun. "What did you steal from him?"

Lenny chuckled "His woman. Long time ago. Not this girl we're going to see."

He drove on, the stake body's headlights illuminating the van's interior. Lenny snatched a look at the side-view. "I got this. One more block." The truck closed to the point its headlights had dropped below the van's windows. Its engine was loud.

On the approach to the next cross street, Lenny flipped on the right signal, but went left. He knew how to drive, turning in short arcs around the steep curve, straightening the wheel as the tires momentarily lost traction, feathering the gas as needed. I looked back. The stake body was already into a broad skid. Its driver fought his way around it, steering into the turn, but couldn't recover and kept on, skidding the opposite way, its rear wheels passing its front, throwing up water like a huge lawn sprinkler on roller skates. It spun out of sight, and I heard an impact as we pulled away on the cross street.

"Asshole. I knew he'd lose it. He shoulda just drove to Quinn's." He looked at the sign in the next intersection. "We gotta double back. That little excursion took us off course." Something blew past the windshield as he pulled into a driveway to K-turn.

"What's Quinn's?"

He motioned past us and said, "Bar over that way. They're open all year." He backed onto the street. "I'd go there, but I'm flagged."

We drove two blocks, until the van lost momentum with the engine still running. Lenny worked the accelerator like it was a kick drum pedal, but there was nothing there. We drifted to a stop and the engine stalled. "Shit." He opened the door to the storm and got out. "God damn it."

I got out the other side. "What is it?

He lay in the water in front of the van and pulled himself under the grill. In a few seconds, he got up and moved to the van's back doors, shaking water from his fingers. "Linkage busted on me." He pulled the doors open and climbed inside. "It broke before. Pin fell out. I cinched it together with ceiling wire and it was working okay, but that must have been too much. Wasn't meant to stand up to drag racing. I think I still got some wire, back here." He rummaged around, looking under pieces of sheetrock and particle board. "Yeah, I knew I had some." He came out with a short, kinked length, less than a foot long.

"Is that enough?"

He got the back doors closed again and said, "I'll make it work." He climbed back underneath. A few seconds later, he pulled himself out and stood. "It's good, now." He wiped his face and said, "You gotta be an engineer to keep this thing running." He shook water from his hands.

Something big flew at me, spinning with the wind. I dropped and it slammed into Lenny, a full sheet of particle board. He lay still in the flooded roadway, his head smashed. The sheet must have hit him on edge. The rain washed blood from the wound, a deep channel running jaw to temple, across one eye. The other seemed to stare at me as I went through his pockets and recovered the van keys. His wallet's bottom edge was held together with duct tape and held eleven dollars. I put the money in my pocket and got into the driver's seat. The van started in a couple tries. I backed up and drove away.

CHAPTER ELEVEN

enny's van stalled the first time I slowed to watch for traffic. I
had to shift to neutral and rev the engine to keep it running.
I came to a big street. The sign read Brigantine Avenue. It
nagged at me. I turned onto it and drove a few blocks, past the
CVS property, surrounded by yellow caution tape. A patrol car
idled on the lee side of the storm, holding the scene. I remembered
Picozzi's birthday card in his kitchen and the return address.
4500 Brigantine. I saw I was heading away and U-turned, the
tires plowing up a wave describing the van's arc. I reasoned a
corner property here unlikely to be a single house.

I was right. It was a broad four-story building of condomini-
ums, set back from the street. It looked older than a lot of the
buildings on the island, and likely had been a fancy hotel con-
verted to fit housing trends. It looked expensive. Its brickwork
was detailed, a lot of coping and arched lintels. A crescent-shaped
driveway led to a gabled porte cochere, fronting the entrance.

There were a handful of cars in its lot. I circled the block,
parked on the side of the building, and trotted through the rain
to its entryway. It was unlikely that she was home, but I needed
to try. I didn't remember her name and searched those listed on
the apartment buzzers and found hers. Di Michael. That was the
name on the envelope's return address. Her first name was Rita.
I pushed her apartment bell. If she were home, she might know
something that could help me get out of this mess, or at least
learn how I got in it. If she was gone, I'd have a safe place to
stay. The glass entrance door had a slim steel plate covering the

TONY KNIGHTON

gap near its lock, making it difficult to slip. I knelt to study it
more carefully and a woman's voice came through the intercom.
"Hello?"

I hadn't expected a response but stood and took a moment to
remember the name on the fake identification. I said, "I'm here
to speak to Maria Chavez."

After a moment, she said, "Why?"

She hadn't asked, 'who's that?' or 'who are you?' so she was
in on Picozzi's dodge, at least enough to know a flat denial would
be pointless. If anything, she sounded annoyed. I believed I knew
better. She must be frightened. I said, "I have pieces of her property that I'd like to return."

She was quiet. I gave her a few more seconds and tried sounding vulnerable. "I also want to ask a favor." It was the truth.

It was still for a few more seconds and the buzzer sounded.
I pushed my way inside and took the stairs to her floor. Midway
down the hall, a door stood slightly ajar. Light shown at the bottom of two other doors.

I knocked twice on hers and pushed inside. She stood in the
kitchen, behind an island. She wore a sweatshirt and jeans but
somehow looked to be a more glamorous person than the one
in the photo. I suppose it had to do with how she carried herself.
"What are you doing here?" She held her right hand below the
island's countertop.

"I need to know who you called just now, Picozzi or the
police?"

She hesitated a moment and must have realized it wouldn't
matter. "Charlie. He didn't pick up. He's probably busy." She sat
on a stool, her right hand still hidden. "I wouldn't call the police
after you said that name. You probably wouldn't be someone they
could help me with. Answer me. What are you doing here?"

There was no point trying to play this woman. "I was at
Picozzi's house, tonight." She knew enough about him to know

he dealt with unpleasant people sometimes. It was part of his business. "He had some things of yours." I lifted my backpack to shoulder height. "There's nothing inside this but some hand tools and an envelope with your things. If you want to look yourself, I'll put it down and step back."

She shook her head. "You knew that name. I know what you have in your bag. What is this? A shakedown?"

"Of course not."

"Never mind of course not. Answer me. What do you want?"

"We're doing it." I gestured around the room. "I want to ride out the worst of the storm."

"Here?"

"Yeah. You don't look like you were going to sleep tonight, anyway. This way, you have company." She didn't seem happy. I said, "I'll stay on my side of the room." I nodded in her direction. "You keep your gun with you, if it makes you feel better."

"Oh, trust me, I will. I know how to use it, too."

Below the bluster, she was frightened. I said, "I don't doubt that." I needed her calm, and added, "I don't hurt people. I'm just a thief." I pointed to her television. "Anything you've heard about me harming anyone is a lie. The truth is I very unintentionally pissed off the wrong guy. Another guy, not Picozzi."

"Charlie's not overjoyed, either."

"No, I don't suppose he would be, but all I was looking for was money. Hurting someone, anyone, doesn't put a dime in my pocket, but it does make the police more interested and that's the last thing I'd want, okay?"

"What if Charlie had walked in on you?"

"I'd bullshit him."

Despite her wariness, she smiled. "What would you say?"

"I was there to fix the refrigerator." I held up my backpack. "If he asked me why I wasn't in the kitchen, I'd tell him there was nothing wrong with the one there, I was looking for another.

When he'd say he hadn't called anyone, I'd say this was the address I had on the work order." As though speaking to him, I said, "It's out in my truck. Come on, take a look." I pointed over my shoulder with my thumb. "Once I'm outside, I'm gone."

She nodded. "So, what else do you want from me?"

"Tell me how involved you are in Picozzi's business?"

She ignored that and said, "Charlie had it drummed into his head to be prepared. Just like a boy scout." She pointed to my backpack. "That envelope was there if he ever had to leave in a hurry." She sat back. "He'd like it if I came with him."

"Would you?"

"I've told him that I don't know." She paused and I thought she had finished her answer, but she said, "I'm very fond of Charlie but the shore has always been my home. I couldn't go anywhere else and have the friends I have here. Places I like to go." She stared at me while she spoke but seemed not to see me, as though she were using the opportunity to make her feelings more clear to herself by voicing them. "It would take too long to start over, somewhere new. Charlie understands what it would mean, what I'd be giving up. He says it's an open offer." She nodded toward the backpack. "We both hope he never has to use those things."

"What do you think? Will he, someday?"

"People say a lot of things about him but honestly, Charlie's not a crook. He's made a lot of money but that was never what it was about, to him. I mean, you've seen his place. He lives well, but not outrageously." She anticipated my next question. "He's owned that property on the beach for over thirty years. Worked out a way to defer the taxes, so he could afford to sit on it. The house, he built about eight, nine years ago. None of it cost him what it's worth but he can show that everything he did was legal. That's how he does everything. Careful. So no, I don't think he'll ever need to use that envelope."

"But it's good to be ready."

"It makes him feel better.?"

She seemed more accepting of the circumstances but still uneasy. I wanted to keep her talking. "How long have you known him?"

"I'm not sure. Charlie was one of those guys who just always seemed to be around but was *easy* to be around, you know? He's fun. Funny. One night, we ended up together. After a while, it was steady. That's been a dozen years, now." She smiled.

"What's that been like?"

She heard something in my question that offended her. "What the hell's that supposed to mean?" Maybe she was more on edge than she showed.

"No, sorry. I mean being with anyone for that long?"

She stared at me for a moment. "Yeah, you couldn't know. Well, if it works, it's good. There's an easiness that only comes with familiarity."

I thought about Susan again and said, "I guess it would." Almost automatically, I added, "I thought I knew what that was like." She waited for me, and I said, "Until a couple days ago."

She knew the answer but said, "What happened?"

I didn't need her to know any more about me and changed the subject. "How did you meet him?"

"I tended bar at Harrah's. The VIP room. Charlie would come by."

"Looking at how he lives, I wouldn't think he was a drinker."

She shook her head. "He goes places to work the crowd—buying rounds, pressing flesh. Nurses a highball all night long. Good tipper. It's what politicians do."

I wanted to know more about why I was in this predicament. "What does that state cop have against him?"

"I have no idea." She seemed to think about what she said, next. "I don't think it matters. It's been my experience that aggressively ambitious people are almost always vindictive, too." She let a tiny smile show and said, "Women are worse than the men."

Her cell phone rang. I looked. It was Picozzi. She was staring at me when I looked back. I said, "Don't answer it." It rang again.

"He'll expect me to. I wouldn't call him on a night like this if it wasn't important."

After the third ring, I said, "There was a loud noise, you thought something hit the building. You got scared, but you're over it now."

She nodded and reached for the phone. I said, "On speaker."

She left the phone on the counter and answered the call, "Hey, Baby."

Picozzi said, "I saw you called. What's up?" There was a lot of background noise on the phone—people talking to be heard over the storm sounds.

"I'm sorry, Charlie, a big piece of wood or something must have smacked into the building. It really scared me but it's all right, nothing happened and I'm fine."

"That's okay. I'm sending somebody to get you out of there."

She said, "No, no, I'm fine right here—"

Picozzi spoke over her. "Yes. The storm changed direction and we're gonna be under water by high tide. There's too much going on. Pack a small bag, we'll have you back home in a day or two." He hung up.

I was disgusted and it must have shown. She looked at me. I said, "You did what you could."

She said, "Look, you can still stay here. I won't say anything."

I chuckled and picked up her phone. "Take your time packing that bag, okay? That's all I'm asking. I've done no more here than keep you company." She seemed about to ask so I held up the phone and said, "I'll leave this somewhere in the open. You'll get it back."

"What about Charlie's money? His cards?"

"I'll mail his cards to him."

She seemed to consider and said, "Go on. You were never here."

I left and made sure to make noise opening the door to the stair. I went down a flight, to the second floor. At the far end of the hall, I tapped on a door with no light behind it. After half a minute of waiting, I let myself inside the condo, put my picks away and went through the rooms quickly, without any light. Then I pulled a kitchen chair near the front window and sat.

Her phone showed me it was 10:59 but that was all. It needed a passcode to open. I turned it off and left it on the windowsill. There wasn't much moving on the street. A few police cars passed without stopping. I could make out the sheets of windblown rain in the glow of the streetlamps. I couldn't hear anything over the storm.

In about ten minutes, a car pulled to a stop by the front entrance. The driver got out and hustled around the car toward the door and disappeared from my line of sight. A few minutes later, he came back outside with Picozzi's woman, running through the rain to the car, and pulled away. I kept watch out the window. The woman owed me nothing and I had no reason to trust her.

As I waited, it occurred to me that she hadn't mentioned anything about Picozzi's card playing. I hadn't asked, but if the man was a degenerate gambler, it was odd she hadn't made some reference. It could be she just didn't want to talk about it with me. It was still odd. She had spoken fondly of the man. Women connected to gambling addicts rarely had a lot of nice things to say about them.

A few minutes later, a police car pulled up out front. Two cops in uniform got out of the car. A third man wore coveralls and a ball cap and carried a small toolbox. He seemed hesitant but ran through the rain toward the front door with the cops.

I couldn't know whether the woman gave me up or Picozzi sensed something was off. It didn't matter. The civilian was either a maintenance man with a master key or a locksmith. The cops meant to go through every apartment in the building. I didn't like that they were expending this level of effort on me in the middle of a storm emergency. For a moment, I thought about staying there and moving behind them to an apartment they'd cleared but rejected the idea as too tricky.

I tugged the backpack over my shoulders, raised the side window and checked. There was nothing moving outside. I straddled the sill, eased my other leg over, hung and dropped, aiming myself to land between two large bushes.

I moved behind one as a set of headlights swept the building. Another police car turned at the corner and drove toward the parking lot in the back. I wouldn't make it back to Lenny's van.

I waited until the cops were out of sight and ran.

CHAPTER TWELVE

A window on the first floor of the church annex showed light. The door opened to an entryway. Perpendicular to that was a hallway, leading to the church proper in one direction. That door was locked. Behind me, somewhere, a chair squeaked.

At the far end of the hall in that direction was a staircase. In between, an open doorway spilled light into the hall. I could hear someone speaking inside the room.

A middle-aged guy came out and said, "Hi. Looking for the meeting?"

"Yeah."

"Well, you found it. Come on in. We just got started."

There were five others inside, three men and two women, sitting in metal folding chairs, facing a desk. All of them stared at me for a moment. The guy said, "Help yourself to coffee. Those doughnuts are left over from the noon meeting but might still be okay." He sat behind the desk and to one of the men sitting, said, "Sorry, Billy. Please, go on."

I took a Styrofoam cup from a stack and tapped the spigot on the coffee maker. It was the color of weak tea. A guy who must have been Billy said, "That's okay, Ray," but nothing else. I palmed two of the powdered supermarket doughnuts and took an empty seat, with a fiftyish woman sitting between Billy and me. On the wall behind him was a poster that read Easy Does It.

He watched as I took almost half a doughnut in one bite, and chewed, the powdered sugar falling across my jacket. It was stale and I washed it down with weak coffee.

Billy held his stare for a moment more and then looked away from me and said, "The big thing I gotta do to stay busy. Most of the guys I come on the job with are retired now but not me and I'm in no hurry. When I *do* go, I'll find something else to do. It's all that works for me, you know? And meetings. I still try to make one a day. You know, I'm working right now, tonight, but I needed a break, get out of the weather for a little bit, so I come here, to the meeting. Used to be, I'd stop somewhere for a drink but none of that no more. I don't know." He looked back at me and away, and said again, "I don't know. I guess that's all I got."

There was a scattered, "Thanks for sharing," from the rest of the people in the room.

A guy sitting on Billy's far side put his hand up. The man who let me in said, "Go ahead, Fred."

Fred said, "Thanks, Ray. I'm Fred, alcoholic. Most of you know me and know about my thing with my daughter. Anyway, today, it's been two years since the last time I heard from her. Like all the kids, now, she doesn't talk on the phone, so I send her texts and emails." A few people chuckled and nodded. "I've asked her to get together with me to talk. I even offered to go to therapy with her if she thinks that might help. Mostly, all I can think of to say is I tell her I love her, and I'd like to talk, anytime she's willing to." Fred seemed overcome and for a moment or two he paused, staring at a spot on the floor as though collecting his thoughts. Finally, he said, "I've come to terms with the idea that this might be it. She might never talk to me again." His voice choked on the last word, and he stopped again. Billy patted his shoulder. Fred took a deep breath and said, "That's all I got. Thanks, guys."

The rest of them said, "Thanks for sharing, Fred."

One of the women said, "Daughters are tough, Freddie."

A few said, "Yeah." Billy stared at me while he patted Fred's shoulder again.

The guy who let me in said, "I apologize for the crosstalk, but I think you're doing all the right things, Fred. Remember to take care of yourself, too." He turned to me and said, "For the benefit of the gentleman who just joined us, Friday nights are usually a topic meeting but what with the storm and all, we're just talking about whatever we got going on, and then we're gonna call it a night." I felt self-conscious, wolfing down stale doughnuts like a bum. The guy noticed my discomfort, broke eye contact and looked around the room. "Anybody else got anything?"

The woman who'd spoken to Fred said, "My name's Arlene and I'm an alcoholic."

The group said, "Hi, Arlene."

"Fred got me thinking. There's no trouble like family trouble. My brother and sister-in-law…"

I was mostly able to tune her out while I thought things over. Bits of things she said got through. "…he never misses the opportunity to take a shot at somebody. I do my best to hold my tongue but it's tough." I thought about Picozzi. Nothing Buddy had told me about him seemed to match the little I'd learned so far. I cursed myself again for my carelessness.

The guy who let me in said, "Excuse me."

I looked up. I'd tuned out everything the woman had said and hadn't noticed she'd finished. I said, "I apologize. I'm a little distracted."

"That's okay," the guy said, "Would you like to share?"

It felt incumbent upon me to. I said, "Sure but look, I'm new to all this and I'm not certain about how I should—what I ought to talk about."

He smiled. "That's okay. Everyone in this room sat in the same place you're in now. Figuratively, I mean."

The other woman said, "There you go with your fifty-cent words again, Ray. You're gonna scare the kid away." A few chuckled.

"He knows what I mean," Ray turned to me and said, "Don't you?"

"Yes, I do."

"Usually, we start by telling each other our name. If you'd like, you could tell us yours."

"Tom," I said. It was the first thing that came to mind. "It's Tom."

The bunch of them said, "Hi, Tom."

Ray said, "Is this your first AA meeting, Tom."

"Yes, it is."

"None of this is organic chemistry, man." he said. "We generally talk about things relating to alcohol and sobriety but that can encompass a lot of life. If you want, just tell us what's on your mind tonight. What brought you here?"

I almost laughed at that question but didn't. It wouldn't be prudent and anyway, I was too tired. Instead, I thought about Susan. "I think my girlfriend broke up with me a couple days ago." This seemed a ready-made dodge, but I paused here, for a moment, unsure how to continue. I smiled and said, "I mean, the tipoff is that tomorrow, she's catching a plane out of town with a one-way ticket."

Most in the room chuckled appreciatively, even Fred.

I said, "Two days ago, Wednesday, she told me she was going. That was the first time I had any idea that there was a problem." I stopped and said, "That's the wrong way to say that. It's the first time I saw that she was unhappy. I don't know why I hadn't noticed. I take pride in being aware—my surroundings, people— it's saved my—" I stopped again and said, "Why was I so unaware of her dissatisfaction?"

The bunch of them nodded. Ray winked at me.

"A few months ago, someone told me that she must be a strong person. I thought about it and agreed with them. I should have thought more about that. I've always considered her someone who's easy to be around, easy to be friends with. I suppose I hadn't given any thought to how difficult I might be." I looked around at the others as I spoke. Most were looking back at me.

Billy was looking down, at something in his hand on the far side of his lap, away from me. His lips moved silently as his forearm was making small movements—he was texting. He finished and slid his phone into his pocket. He saw me watching him as he looked up and quickly looked away.

I kept talking. "I mean, my life—sometimes I don't even know why I do the things I do. Most of the time, I'm as regular, as normal as anyone else. Pragmatic. I suppose I haven't wanted to be self-analytical. Maybe I'm missing something, missing some part that other people have—" I caught myself. I was getting lost in pointless rumination and needed to focus. I took a breath and said, "I apologize. I'm rambling and I'm not sure what else I have to say. Thanks."

"That's fine, Tom." He looked around and said, "I think that's everybody. Is anyone here dying to take a drink? No? Okay, then. We have a nice way of closing."

He came out from behind the desk and the rest stood, some moving to take each other's hands. The woman next to me moved away, toward Fred. "Martha's coming to my house for coffee, Fred. Why don't you come with us?"

Billy closed the gap between us. He held his far hand behind him. He smelled of smoke. I stomped on his instep and punched him in the stomach. He doubled over. I brought my knee up, hard, into his face. His teeth came together with an audible *click,* and he fell, out. A set of handcuffs landed on the floor next to him.

The others stood there, shocked. I bent down, took the phone from his jacket pocket, and was patting him down for his gun when Ray put his hand on my shoulder and turned me around. He was strong. "Jesus, Fella, what was that for?"

I stood and faced him down for a moment. No one in the room moved. I grabbed my backpack and ran back outside, into the storm and away from a swiftly approaching car running without headlights.

CHAPTER THIRTEEN

The homes in these blocks were mostly big triplexes. The builder had packed them in as tightly as he could. There was room enough between them for a family to walk to the back door if they traveled single file.

I ducked between two. Billy's phone came to life without a pass code. As I'd imagined, his last text read, *He's here.* He'd sent it to a group of six—three phone numbers and three names, Lloyd, Robby and Bluff. There were other messages, the last from Bluff, that read, *APB out. We need 2 B 1ˢᵗ.* I thought about that and didn't like it, but it wouldn't change what I had to do. I looked at Billy's earlier texts, but none seemed significant.

There was a blue plastic five-gallon recycling bucket in the walkway. I turned it over and sat. Even cold and wet, it felt good. Too good. I'd stiffen up if I sat too long. I ran my hand across face and shook water from my fingers. I was angry but only with myself, and only because I hadn't prepared. Buddy had made no bones about not knowing more than he'd said. I'd had two days to learn what I should have known about Picozzi before I came here, tonight, but I hadn't. I'd let my personal life intrude upon business.

A small part of me wanted to be angry with Susan for that, angry because she'd sprung this, no notice, no real discussion. Realistically, a discussion wouldn't have resolved anything. She hadn't kept me from preparing.

The more I rested the better I was feeling. It was likely that no amount of homework would have prepared me for tonight's police response. It was odd that a bunch of ranking state cops were taking in a local department's routine dispatch, and on the night of a bad storm. Alarm systems were scut work—lots of cops sought promotion to avoid those calls.

I was about to pitch the phone when it occurred to me that I might have a way to improve my chances—maybe even end this nonsense entirely. It might have been my underlying foul mood that gave me this idea, but it felt like a good move. If I was right, I'd have to work quickly.

A house on the next corner was dark on all three floors. I banged on the door to the first-floor apartment, waited a few seconds and kicked it in. I tried the light switch; the power was on. The apartment seemed furnished in a combination of Ikea table and chairs and a yard-sale sofa. There was a cheap floor lamp in the front corner of the living room.

I put Billy's phone on the coffee table, picked up a few cardboard coasters, wedged shut the front door, and pulled on it, as a test. It held well enough in the ruined doorframe. The floor lamp's cord was long. I pitched its shade, set the lamp in front of the door and switched it on.

In the kitchen, I turned the stove knobs full open, past the clicking quartz lighters. Unlit gas hissed from the burners. The odor followed me out the back door as I pulled it shut, locking it.

I ran through the walkway to the front, across the street, between two homes, and stood behind those, on the far side of the block. I waited.

I was beginning to think I'd figured this wrong when a black Chrysler pulled up in front of the house I'd rigged. I'd been right. Bluff's crew had trackers on their phones. They'd followed Billy's here. Four men got out of the car. I was too far away to see if Bluff was with them, but I hoped he was. If he was putting up the money to find me, the pursuit might end here.

Two crept into the walkway, toward the rear, pistols in hand. The men out front waited for them to get into place, and one tried to open the front door with his free hand. He pushed a couple times, but it was too tightly wedged shut. He stepped back, kicked the door just below its knob and it flew open.

For a moment, it seemed only that someone had turned on all the lights at once, but then the concussion blew out the walls, with a deep-sounding *Crump!* that I felt through the soles of my shoes, followed by a clatter of falling debris that lasted longer than seemed reasonable. A huge fireball rolled and twisted its way up through the storm and was gone, leaving flames coming from the settling debris. The Chrysler was resting on its roof.

Cautiously, I went toward it all. The three-story house had been reduced to a one-story-high pile of burning rubble. At its top, a fiberglass tub enclosure, supported only by its supply and drainpipes, swayed in the wind. The house next door was ablaze and appeared to be heavily damaged, as well. Debris littered the intersection. Shards of broken glass sparkled like thousands of tiny diamonds, reflecting the flames.

There was movement down the street. A man was trying to stand or at least crawl. He must have been blown clear. I ran through the rain and pushed him over onto his back to search him for a gun. His clothes were tattered. I checked his ankles for a holster. His bare feet were scorched—he'd been blown out of his shoes. He kept trying to say something as I frisked him. I couldn't find anything useful. The weapon he'd carried when the house blew must have been all he'd had. As I took his wallet, he grabbed my wrist with his blackened fingers. Through what was left of his mouth, I heard him croak out, "How do I look?"

The man was dead, he just didn't know it yet. Sirens sounded in the distance. I shook free of his grip and took off down the street.

CHAPTER FOURTEEN

I stuffed the cop's money into my pocket without counting and pitched his wallet. Hitting back at my pursuers had given me a better feeling about my chances. It might have accounted for why I was in the open when a white Cadillac sedan running without its headlights turned onto the street in front of me. I cursed my carelessness as it slowed to a stop. Both widows on my side came down and the man up front said, "What are you doing?"

"Trying to get inside somewhere." I pointed my thumb over my shoulder. "My car stalled out a few blocks over that way."

"Who are you?"

These were the guys I'd seen come over the bridge, minus one. Maybe one of the guys I'd tangled with in the parking garage. I stepped closer, said, "Here you go, fellas," and reached toward my pocket.

The man in the backseat brought up a pistol, too fast. He seemed high-strung. The man up front noticed and said, "Easy, Frankie."

I held my hands out, away from my body, fingers spread and said, "I'm only going to take my wallet out and show you who I am."

The guy in the front seat nodded. "Go on."

I took it out and opened it two-handed to show them the badge.

"You Philly?"

"Yeah."

"What are you doing here?"

"Probably the same as you. I got a call from one of Bluff's guys. I was already down here, in North Cape May. I made it up all right but took a bad turn back there and my car flooded out and died."

"Which one of Bluff's guys called you?"

"Billy."

He waited. I thought of the rest of the names in the text chain and said, "I know Billy, and there's Lloyd and Robby, but those are the only guys I ever met. I'm from Philadelphia."

The man up front nodded and said, "Come on, then, get in." Frankie, in back, opened his door. I got into the car as he moved over. The driver took his foot off the brake, and we rolled down the street. I didn't like this but there was nothing else to do. It was good to get out of the weather, at least.

Frankie, next to me, said, "You seen that explosion back there? Lit up the whole sky."

"Yeah, I did. What was that?"

"Couldn't tell. We were too far away."

The man up front said, "Like I said, probably a transformer."

Frankie said, "That musta been one big fucking transformer. It lit up the whole sky."

The driver said, "I still don't know about that, John. There's lights on all around here, still."

I thought it good to engage with these men, and said, "Most places, power is fed from both directions, so service is maintained."

John said, "See? What'd I say?" He half-turned in his seat and continued, addressing me. "That's what I told these guys." He faced front and said, "That's why downed lines are so dangerous. They could still be live."

The driver said, "Yeah, John, I know, but all the power here comes from inland—one direction, you know?"

"Look, I don't have time to explain it to you, so don't argue. Let's keep our eye on the ball."

"Sure, John. I'm just saying."

John said to me, "How you know Bluff?"

I improvised. "I met him down here a while ago, at a thing. It turned out we knew some of the same guys. My uncle's Eddie Bishop, 401's Business Agent, you know? Bluff knows him. Since then, we've helped each other out a couple times."

That seemed to satisfy him. The driver said, "What's 401?"

"Ironworkers Local."

"Right, right."

The guy next to me said, "You shoulda got your uncle to hook you up, man. Ironworkers make *sick* money."

"I'm afraid of heights."

The driver and Frankie laughed. John said, "Yeah, fuck that shit. That's hard fucking work."

The wind gusted and rain pounded the windshield. The driver slowed to a crawl and said, "I don't know about this, John." He leaned close to the windshield and turned the wipers on high. It didn't seem to help.

John said, "Just take it easy. We'll be all right."

The driver said, "We been at this a while now and we ain't seen nobody on the street, yet."

John pointed his thumb over his shoulder at me and said, "We saw this guy, didn't we?"

"Yeah, and his car stalled out. We're taking a chance here, is all I'm saying."

"We're gonna keep looking till somebody turns him up. I want this prick, myself."

"Me too, John. What the fuck, Moochy's my first cousin, you know? I just mean I think this guy is probably holed-up somewhere."

"I don't care what you think, Chucky. Bluff asked for help and we're helping him. So just shut up and drive."

"Sure, John, sure. I'm just saying, is all." He waited a beat and said, "I still gotta get back tonight." John didn't say anything, and the driver added, "Sometime soon, you know?"

"I heard you before, Chucky. Like I said, we're staying with this until it's done."

"I know you said, John, but I'm nervous about that thing."

"Buddy's always been good pay. He'll take care of you."

I'd been thinking my own thoughts, only half-listening to their small talk but now I wanted to hear everything. Chucky said, "He's been off the air since Wednesday." He waited for a reply that didn't come and added, "Over two days, now."

"I know how long ago Wednesday was."

"It's not like him, is all. He usually picks up or calls back, quick. Within the hour, at least."

"He probably got out of town after doing his bit. Anyway, this don't sound like a me problem, it sounds like a you problem. Bluff asked for help, we're helping him. Understand?"

Chucky wasn't happy but said, "Sure, John, sure."

We traveled a couple blocks in silence. I was working out how I'd get free of these guys. Frankie said, "Hey, John, what kind of name is Bluff, anyway? Irish?"

The two up front broke into loud laughter. John said, "Frankie, did you get dropped on your head?"

Chucky said, "It's a nick-name, you moron."

"Hey, fuck you." Frankie was more embarrassed than angry. "It's a weird name. How am I supposed to know?"

"It *is* weird," Chucky said. "How'd he get that name, John?"

"It's a long story."

"We got time. We're just riding around, looking."

John was silent for a few moments and said, "I don't even know how true it is. I heard when he was a rookie, they partnered him with this old-timer, Falcone. Falcone had been on the pad forever—"

Chucky said, "He any relation to Bobby Falcone?"

"No." John sounded testy. He didn't like being interrupted, and said, as though to a slow child, "Bobby's from Philly. Mayfair. Okay?

"Sure, John. Sorry."

John said, "Falcone the *cop* made collections and what-not. Good guy but a little shaky. Bluff seemed okay, so Falcone laid it out for him, and Bluff was in. Beautiful. Good for Falcone, good for us. Like I said, though, Falcone was always a little shaky. The way I heard it, one day, these two Feds brace them on the street—"

"Hey," Frankie said, "slow up, slow up. I seen something moving over there." He was looking through his window. He sounded keyed-up.

Chuckie slowed to a stop and looked but said, "I don't see nothing. What do you think, John?"

I saw an opportunity and said to Frankie, "Let's get out and have a look." To the two up front, I said, "You guys circle the block."

"No," John said, "no, youse two sit tight, but yeah, take us around the block, Chucky. Everybody keep your eyes open."

"Okay, boss." Chucky made the turn and drove slowly.

We made a circuit. Frankie said, "I swear I seen something."

John said, "I think you saw the wind moving something, Frankie, but that's okay, you're staying sharp."

"Thanks, John."

"Keep going this way, Chucky."

We rode for a block and Chucky said, "So what about Bluff?"

"Huh? Yeah, right. Two Feds roll up on them and tell them somebody on their route flipped, they'll testify, they got recordings, the works. This is it, give us some names or you're going to jail. Falcone folds up. He's pissing himself, says he'll do whatever they want." John chuckled again. "Bluff shoves him and starts yelling something like, 'Shut the fuck up. They got nothing. It's a bluff. They'd have a warrant if they had something. It's nothing but a bluff.' He tells the Feds to go fuck themselves, gets his commander on the radio and tells him—basically, tells every cop in the state—the same story, it's a bluff and he wants his union rep. Turned out, he was right, they had shit. He's been Bluff ever since."

"Good story," Frankie said.

"Yeah. If it's true, yeah," John pointed and said, "Turn right, up here, Chucky."

Frankie said, "Sounds like he's got balls."

"Yes, he does."

Chucky said, "You think that guy got Picozzi's money, John?"

John said, "What money?"

"Everybody says he's got a pile, hidden in his house, somewheres. Maybe a million bucks."

"I heard that too," said John. "I don't believe it for a second."

"Why not?"

"Picozzi's not like us. He don't even carry cash. Pays for everything with a card." We approached an intersection before the street dead-ended at the bay. Chucky threw his turn signal on. John said, "Besides, that whole thing was a set-up." Chucky made the turn. John leaned closer to the windshield. "You guys see anything moving up here?"

I saw my chance. "Yeah, off to the right, there? Yeah. Looks like somebody ducked back behind that house."

"All right let's go. Chucky, let us out and go around the block, cut him off." We rolled to a stop in front of the house, and I piled out of the car with the others. John pulled a gun and pointed to a driveway. "Hey, Philly, you and Frankie go that way." He hadn't noticed that my hands were empty, and trotted toward another driveway, two doors down.

Eager to please his boss, Frankie took off running. I let him get ahead of me and stayed a couple steps behind. My plan was to get out of sight of the other two, drop Frankie and take his pistol. He slowed at the corner of the house and looked. I came up behind him, but he turned and hissed, "Quiet, man." He sounded anxious.

I nodded, and he went around the corner to the back of the house. I made the turn. Two houses away, a security light popped on, revealing a silhouette. I said, *"There he is."*

Startled, Frankie fired three times. The man grunted and fell, and Frankie said, "Oh, shit, it's John," and ran to him, crying, "Oh, fuck, oh fuck."

For a second, I thought about following and taking his gun but doubled back and kept moving.

CHAPTER FIFTEEN

I worked my way far from the mobsters, along the bay side of the island and was in an area of homes smaller and more ordinary than other places I'd seen tonight. A block farther on was a small bar. Its only lights were inside, a soft glow that shown past the darkened beer neons in its front windows. An unlit sign fronting its porch roof reading Quinn's shook in the wind. This was the place that Lenny, the copper thief had mentioned. I pushed my way through the rain, up the porch steps, struggled to open the door and got inside.

A little more than a dozen people were there. This wasn't the kind of place that attracted summer vacationers. These were permanent residents. A few turned to see who'd come in and went back to watching the news.

From somewhere behind the bar, a woman's voice said, "Sorry, we're closed."

Another woman, a patron, at the far end, said, "Jesus, Marie, let him in. It's bad out there." She sounded like either a smoker or whiskey-drinker but had the kind of female voice that carried, even at low volume.

A man at the bar voiced agreement. "Come on. Give the guy a break."

I stood there a moment, dripping on the floor. The bartender was a red-haired woman who was maybe seventy. She looked me over and said, "Yeah, come on in."

The younger woman spoke to the bartender, continuing a story. "He'd have kept us there all night if we hadn't sold out of everything." She sounded a little drunk and sat sideways with her back against the wall, facing the door. She rested a bottle of beer on her knee, holding it by the neck. "He tried to sell a guy the pallets." She stared at me as she took a pull on her beer.

The bartender laughed and said, "Oh, my god," as she poured a patron a shot. A guy at the bar shrugged with a silent chuckle but kept watching the television.

I walked past a table, where a guy who sounded like an accountant was in conversation with a middle-aged couple— something about property taxes.

I thought I might be able to make something happen. A seat at the bar was empty, between a guy with a utility knife sheathed on his belt and the boozy woman. She finished her beer and continued telling the bartender about her boss. "He'd have lost the place a long time ago if it wasn't for me." Noting my approach, she swung her legs forward to make room and set her empty on the bar. "The latest is he wants to put us on this lousy plan that has a forty-dollar deductible for office visits." She had a worn, silver bracelet on her wrist with *Angela* engraved on it.

The bartender took the empty and said to me, "Be right with you, Hon," then, "That's a sin."

I sat with my foot on the backpack and surveyed the patron's reflections in the mirror behind the bottles. Besides the woman next to me and the couple, the remaining customers were men who looked to be contractors. One, sat at the middle of the bar, in front of the taps, seemed familiar. A few of them muttered things to each other but most seemed to be there to drink and watch news of the storm. The television volume was too low to hear.

I'd created enough chaos in the past hour to have bought some time but eventually, someone would look here. The patrons could be a problem. While none would likely pay much attention to me, they'd remember I'd come in. My being here wasn't smart, but I needed a break, a few minutes out of the wind and rain.

My rough idea was to follow one of these guys when they left, jack their car and find somewhere sheltered to park and ride it out. The woman next to me, Angela, met my eyes in the mirror. She was heavily made up but pretty.

The bartender brought her another beer and put a coaster on the bar in front of me. "What can I get you?"

I put a ten on the bar and said, "Just a club soda, please."

"Lime?"

"Sure. Hey, do you have any peanuts or something like that?"

"Just some packs of those Lance crackers."

"Could I have a couple packs of the peanut butter?"

"You got it, Kiddo."

She moved away to get them. Angela's leg brushed mine as she shifted in her seat.

The CVS showed on the television. I heard a man say, "I'll take another, when you get a chance, Marie."

"Okay, Rory."

His voice sounded familiar. I looked again and realized he was the guy who had been driving the stake body truck I'd jumped into earlier. And who'd chased Lenny's van. I hadn't seen his truck outside. He drank off what was left in his bottle, put it down next to an empty shot glass and idly stroked his Fu Manchu while he watched the news. I supposed he hadn't seen my face clearly enough on the dark street to recognize me now, but I needed to be careful. As Marie brought him another beer and refilled his shot glass, I shifted on my stool slightly in Angela's direction to where a bottle on the top shelf blocked his reflection.

There was footage showing the remains of the house I'd blown up and some fire apparatus. The banner underneath the picture read Natural Gas Explosion—Three Believed Dead. The man next to me said, "I wondered what that was. That's rough." He was turned away and continued talking with two others about a job he'd left late this afternoon. "I got it buttoned up pretty good, but weather like this, you always worry, you know?"

The wind gusted outside, changing direction. It felt like the building flexed slightly, in response. Everyone in the bar sat up. I turned as rain dashed against the front windows like someone had cracked open a firehose. In a moment, the wind reverted, and a moment after that we relaxed. A few chuckled. The man next to me said, "If I'm lucky, maybe the whole place'll collapse and he'll never know the plywood blew away." His friends and some others laughed. His keys were on the bar in front of him, along with a bottle of Sierra Nevada and change. The guy on his far side said something I couldn't make out.

The television screen showed a long shot of Picozzi's house, surrounded by police vehicles. Caution tape jerked in the wind. The banner read "County Executive Picozzi's Home Burglarized." Below that another read, "Police Officer Hospitalized in Serious Condition."

The bartender put my drink and the crackers in front of me and said to Angela, "Dave gets ours through the county but it's not so great, either." She picked up my ten.

Angela said, "What're you gonna do?" and drank from her bottle.

The bartender nodded and walked away to take another order. I tore open the first pack with my teeth and ate one of the crackers. They were stale.

Angela said, "How about you?"

It took me a moment to realize she was talking to me. "Health insurance?"

"Yeah."

I said, "I have a part-time job that lets me buy in. It's a good plan but expensive." She looked older than me, late thirties, probably, and seemed interested in my answer, even though this was only small talk. "The money I earn there barely covers the premiums."

"Shame, isn't it?" She took a big swallow. "What do you do?"

"The part-time gig isn't very interesting." I held up the crackers and said, "Sorry. I haven't eaten anything since lunch. Have some?"

She waved that away. "No thanks. What else?"

I was lost for a second, then said, "Full time, I'm a contractor." Which, in a way, was true. As I ate a cracker, I said, "How about you?"

She ignored that and brushed cracker crumbs from my jacket. "That what brought you out, tonight?" There was a wet ring on the knee of her jeans, from her last beer.

"Thanks. I'm a slob." I looked up and said, "Yeah."

"You local?"

"No, I'm up there, past Trenton." I pointed my thumb over my shoulder and popped another cracker into my mouth.

The bartender set my change in front of me.

Angela said, "You're cutting it close if you're going home tonight."

"It's worse than that. I travelled down here with a guy to prep his house for the storm while he took care of something else. He was supposed to come back for me." I looked at the others' reflections in the mirror. None were making a move to leave. "But he called half an hour ago and said he was having trouble and wouldn't be getting back."

Angela said, "That's a shame." She seemed genuinely sympathetic. She glanced away as she took a pull on her beer and gave a start. I turned to see. The picture on the television had changed. Picozzi stood in an office that could have been anywhere. With no expression on his face, he spoke, unheard by us, into a microphone. Angela called to the bartender, "Marie, could you turn this up, please?"

"Sure, Doll."

Marie aimed a changer at the screen and thumbed up the volume, catching Picozzi in mid-sentence: "...Mays Landing, where I am best able to facilitate delivery of emergency services to the citizens of Atlantic County. I've been in contact with the governor. He has been supportive and is working to have the entirety of the New Jersey shore declared a federal disaster area. Once transportation is possible, I'll personally undertake an inspection tour of the county, concentrating on but not limited to our shore communities, to assess damage and allocate resources. As always, the safety of our citizens is paramount.

"The other issue that I want to address is the burglary of my home, early this evening. From what I've learned so far, the damage to my property was minimal and nothing seems to have been taken. What most concerns me is the resulting state police response. State troopers forced entry to my home without a warrant. It might be decided at some future date that their claims of probable cause have merit, but the troopers remained inside my home long past the point that they had ascertained there were no persons present, which constitutes a clear violation of the law. I find this invasion of my privacy outrageous and suspicious. These trooper's actions were also a clear jurisdictional violation and possibly criminal. I am therefore personally offering a twenty-thousand-dollar reward for either or both the safe apprehension of the perpetrator of this break-in, and any credible, useful information pertaining to this outrage. Thank you."

Reporters shouted questions as Picozzi turned and left the room. The anchor came on screen. "A rare public statement from County Executive Picozzi. We'll keep you up to the minute on this story along with news of the storm."

The picture on the television had changed. A reporter in a rain slicker and hood held a microphone and spoke to the camera.

Angela nodded and said, "Thanks, Marie." To me, she said, "That guy owned a place I used to work."

The bartender muted the set. "They say he's got a pile of money in that house. I wonder if the robber got it." No one commented. The bartender's phone rang. She answered, "Hey, what's up?"

I wanted to know more about Picozzi and said to Angela, "Where was that? Where you worked?"

She looked away and seemed to be reading the label on her beer bottle. "It wasn't that interesting." She looked back at me and said, "I guess you'll have to ride out the night in his house?" I must have looked blank, and she added, "The house you closed up."

I said, "Already dropped his keys through the slot when I was finished. I went out looking to get something to eat. The guy called after that."

I heard the bartender say, "That sucks," and I looked, but she was still speaking to someone on the phone.

I looked back at Angela and said, "I suppose I'll have to break back in, somehow."

"Oh, no. After all the work you did."

She'd made a simple statement of fact but something in her affect had changed. I realized she could be a way off the street. I smiled and said, "It's okay. I did a shitty job."

She barked a laugh. In the bar mirror's reflection, I saw a couple of the men glance in our direction and away again. She said, "You're a funny guy."

The bartender ended her call and raised her voice, "I gotta close up."

There was a collective groan, and a few men began to protest. The bartender said, "No. Sorry, Dave has to work late now, so I got to get home and let the dogs out. So they can do their business without floating away."

A few grumbled. Two guys stood up and finished their drinks. One said, "Night, Marie. Stay dry." They left.

Angela's beer was already nearly empty. I caught the bartender's eye and said, "Do I have time to get this nice lady another?" I pushed my change forward.

Angela put her hand on mine and said to the bartender, "No, I'm gonna get going, Marie," and to me, said, "Thanks. You're sweet." She finished her beer and said, "Keep me company outside while I grab a smoke." She stood and picked up her change minus a five. "Come on."

"Sure." I picked up my backpack.

She looked past me and waved to Marie. "Good night, Girlfriend. Stay dry."

"You too, Doll."

I left my change on the bar and followed Angela. I stole a glance at Rory as I went past. He was watching us in the mirror's reflection, but nothing showed on his face. He looked drunk.

The bartender called, "See you, fellas," to another bunch, leaving with us. I glanced back. She was clearing our places and said to me, "Thank you." A few still in the bar took note as we walked outside together.

Angela said, "Whoa, it's gotten bad out here."

One of the men coming outside with us said, "See you, Ange," as they dashed down the stairs and up the street, through the rain, to their truck.

She and I stood against the building's wall, to the side of the front door. The porch was on the sheltered side of the wind, but I still felt it. Water in the street had overflowed the gutters in places. The roadway's crown was barely visible. Another guy came out and trotted down the steps and away, to a Dodge Ram.

Angela tore open a pack of Camel Filters, took one in her lips and tried to light it with a red Bic that wouldn't stay lit. Putting a hand on my shoulder, she turned me toward her. "Stay there." She got the cigarette going, took a deep drag and faced the street again, backed against the wall, her shoulder touching mine. As she exhaled, she held the cigarette aloft, her elbow resting on the hand of her free arm, which was tucked under her breasts. "Thanks." She was almost as tall as me. A few more guys stepped out onto the porch, got their keys out and ran into the street, to their cars. One waved. She smiled and fluttered her fingers at him.

Rory came outside, too, stepped onto the porch unsteadily and took a moment to gather himself. Angela said, "You all right, Rory?"

He took a few more seconds but said, "Yeah," without looking at us. He took a pouch from his pocket, pulled a wad of tobacco from it and pushed it into the side of his mouth. He made it down the stairs and away up the street.

I wanted to hear about him and said, "He doesn't look all right."

"Nice guy but a bad drunk. Marie doesn't like to over-serve him, but he always walks home and anyway, if she cuts him off, he pitches a fit."

We were misted by the wet wind, there, under the porch roof. As I watched, a car drove past at about five miles per hour. Its tires sent up a wake that crested over the sidewalks on either side of the street. I thought about Susan but said, "Are you staying in town tonight?"

"Yeah." She saw her cigarette was getting too wet to smoke. She tried one more drag and pitched it away. "I don't leave unless they come around and make me. It *is* looking bad, though. *Shit.*"

"What?"

"I got dropped off, here. Could you—oh, right, you don't have a car, either. Great."

"How far do you have to go?"

"Just a few blocks but I hate getting my hair wet. It takes forever to dry out."

I stripped off my jacket. "Here," I said, holding it out to her, "put this over your head."

She looked at me, waiting for me to give her a reason. I said, "It's only going to be harder, the longer you wait."

The couple hustled outside and was away, down the street. Angela said, "I might still get a ride," and nodded at the front door.

She'd likely known the men inside for years. I said, "Yeah, you might." If she'd wanted a ride from anyone in the bar, she wouldn't be talking to me.

She said, "What are *you* gonna do?"

"I'll go back where I was and break in. Like I said."

She stared for another moment and took my jacket. "Okay." She held it over her head. "Let's go, then." She ran down the porch steps, laughing and screaming, and up the street. I slung the backpack over my shoulders and followed, catching up in a dozen steps. I was soaked and cold again.

CHAPTER SIXTEEN

We ran through the storm, on the sidewalks for three blocks, splashing across two flooded streets, past a house with a piece of loose vinyl siding on its front that was snapping in the wind.

Angela stopped at a small, one-story frame bungalow stood on brick footers. It looked older than the homes around it—maybe pre-WWII construction. Its exterior walls were sided with mossy asbestos tiles. Water covered my shoes to the ankles. She pulled open the screen door and stood on the first of two steps to dig through her purse for keys. The hinges squeaked as she pushed the door open to let us in.

She dropped her bag and keys on a wooden mail table and hung my jacket on a clothes tree. Next to that, an aluminum softball bat stood propped in the corner. My jacket dripped on the entryway linoleum as she turned on the ceiling light, dimming it to a soft glow. This wasn't a cheap summer rental, but a real house. It looked comfortable—lived in. There was a couch and coffee table, a cream-colored beanbag chair, and a television sitting on a short cabinet of drawers. Next to the TV was a cactus in a six-inch clay flowerpot. Above that, a battery-powered dial clock was mounted on the wall.

"Your place is really cool."

"Thank you." She looked around as though seeing it anew. I could tell she was pleased. "Hang on," she said as she kicked her shoes off, "I'll get you a towel," and walked down the hall, past a couple bedrooms and into the bathroom. "Take your shoes off."

At the end of the hallway, kitchen cabinets and the back door were visible. Through the panes in its upper half, I saw the silhouette of a small tree bent halfway over in the wind.

I left my shoes and socks in the entryway, stepped into the living room and pulled the shade away from the window frame a few inches. Except for the storm, the street was quiet. The other houses I could see were dark and likely empty. Windblown rain ran up the street in sheets. Water covered everything, with only the wind intermittently revealing an impression of curb lines.

She called from the kitchen, "All I have to drink is beer and water."

"Oddly enough, water is perfect," I said. She chuckled.

I looked around. The art on her walls wasn't seascapes and driftwood, they were real pictures of real things. There was a pen and ink drawing of a leafless mulberry in winter, its branches gnarled and twisted, another in pastel of three asparagus spears, and what looked like a portrait of the woman herself, maybe when she was younger.

She came in with a beer for herself and a towel and bottle of water for me. She made to hand over both but stopped and said, "I'm sorry, you said you hadn't eaten. I've got some leftover Chinese in the refrigerator." She handed me the bottle and towel.

I dried my face and hair. "That sounds delicious."

"I'll heat it up. It'll just take a minute."

She walked toward the kitchen, and I followed her. "Thanks, Angela."

"Oh, my god, I don't even know your name. You must think I'm such an asshole."

"Not at all." I gave her the first name I thought of. "It's Pete."

"I'm sorry, Pete. Would you like a glass?"

"This is fine." There were more pictures in the kitchen, mostly pastels.

She said, "I should have asked."

I said, "No worries," and pointed to one of the paintings. "Are these yours?"

"Yeah," she said, as she dug white take-out cartons from the refrigerator. "They are."

"They're very good." I blotted my shirt with the towel.

She smiled. "Thank you." She put the cartons into a microwave and pushed buttons. The oven hummed. "Most people don't notice."

"Have you ever sold any of your work?"

"Yeah, some things, here and there. Yeah. These are pieces I'm sort of happy with." She looked around at them. "I haven't done anything lately—we've been pretty busy at work—but I need to start something new. I always feel better when I'm working on something."

The microwave buzzed. She took out the cartons and dumped rice and something with chicken and vegetables into a bowl. "Here, I ate earlier. You go ahead. It's awful when your blood sugar drops." She took the towel and pulled a kitchen chair out for me.

I didn't argue and sat at the table. "Thanks." Its top and edge were covered with white Formica, with little boomerang shapes in light blue.

She looked out the back window. "I'm worried about my little magnolia."

I watched for a moment as the tree was buffeted by the wind, said, "There aren't many trees around here," and began to eat. It was still cold in spots, but I didn't care and ate without tasting.

"There aren't many on the island, at all. That's my baby."

I finished in less than a minute and put the bowl and fork into the sink to wash them, but she said, "Leave it. Come on."

I followed her back into the living room. She touched my arm and said, "Hang on a minute," and went back to the closet for a blanket. "This sofa's nothing special, but we're both a little damp." I helped her spread the blanket over it, an over-sized couch, the kind that became popular in the nineties for furnishing McMansions. She said, "Have a seat," set her phone on the coffee table and sat with her back to the arm of the couch, one leg up, crossed over the other and lit a candle with the Bic. "We're liable to lose power."

I sat and said, "Does that happen a lot," thinking a darkened causeway and bridge might help me off the island.

"More often than I like. The weather beats us up, here."

"But you stay, anyway." I took a drink from the plastic bottle of water.

"Yeah." She gave me a weak smile. "We're a strange bunch, us year-rounders. We bitch about the weather when it's bad but don't have time to enjoy it when it's nice. We're dependent on summer visitors but we resent them. The quiet's nice." She put her hand on my knee. "It's good for me." She picked up a remote. "I want to keep an eye on the weather, if you don't mind."

"No, go ahead."

She clicked it on. A commercial for a car was playing. "I'll keep the sound off." She hiked herself over to close the gap between us.

I didn't know what Susan's plans were, but she likely wouldn't waste time before making friends once she got to Saint John. I set the bottle on a coaster and put my arm around Angela's shoulders. "How long have you been here, Angela?"

"I bought this house five—no, six years ago."

"How long at the shore?"

The commercial ended and a woman reporter in a rain slicker appeared on screen. Angela said, "Let's check this for a minute," and thumbed up the sound with the remote. The reporter was standing on a beach with lights from a casino behind her, while she shouted into the microphone, something about windspeeds and a storm tide. I tried to concentrate—I needed to concentrate more, about the weather, and what it might mean for me, but again, the personal intruded on the practical and I thought about Susan, instead of paying attention.

The banner under the newsman changed and read Two Dead, Multiple Injuries in Shootout. "A CVS drugstore was the scene of a deadly shootout, earlier tonight. Local police and Atlantic County Sheriffs exchanged gunfire with three men who allegedly broke into the Pharmacy—"

Angela thumbed off the sound. "Well, that wasn't very helpful." She smiled at me and said, "We've had a lot of rain the last couple weeks, so the ground is saturated. I think they're overcautious, but that's me. Sorry, I don't have a boat."

I chuckled. "That's okay."

Footage of cops sweeping the CVS parking lot with flashlights showed on the screen, along with caution tape and evidence markers. I'd have liked to hear what they had to say about it, but it really didn't matter. I asked Angela, again, "How long have you been at the shore?"

"Oh, right. Sorry. Ever since high school. The summer I graduated I got a job at the Wildwood Convention Center. I met a guy and stayed after the season ended. I liked it here, the way it emptied out in the fall. He broke up with me that winter, the week before Valentine's Day. Cheap asshole. By then, I'd moved down here for good. He had different plans." Her hand moved up my leg. "I work at a building supply, now."

Someone knocked on the door. She stood and parted the blinds, said, "Fuck," and stepped away from the window.

I didn't know how this would play out but said, "I can leave through the back, if you need me to."

She shook her head and put a hand up but seemed focused on whoever was outside.

The knocking came again, and a man said, "Come on, Angel, open up. I can see you in there."

She looked at me and said softly, "This is a friend but he's not special, okay?"

I nodded.

"I'm not going to let him in, but I'd still rather not get into any drama."

I picked up my shoes and backpack and brought them into the first bedroom off the hallway. I heard the front door squeal open. Over the sounds of the storm, a man said, "What's the matter? Aren't we friends anymore?" His voice sounded familiar.

"Sure, we are."

"You saw it was me. What's up?"

"I'm tired. That's all. What do you want?"

"Just looking out for you. Storm's getting worse."

"I'm fine."

"Good. That's good." There was a pause and he said, "Want me to stop by later on? See how you're doing?"

"I don't think so. Like I said, I'm tired."

"New jacket?"

It threw me for a moment, but I realized he was looking at mine, dripping, there on the clothes tree. I pulled on my shoes.

She went with it. "Yeah. Look, I'm gonna call it a night."

He chuckled. "Come on, who you got in there? Geno?"

"All right, that's enough."

"Don't close the door in my face."

I took the pry bar out of my backpack. Beyond everything else that had gone wrong tonight, I wasn't going to waste time with either of them if he pushed his way past her.

She said, "You gotta go, Jim."

I heard the door squeak but not shut, and he said, "I'm just trying to look out for you."

"I don't need looking after. Let go of the door."

I heard a blast of static, and then a radio transmission. *"We're on location at 5th Street near Evans Boulevard. There's a two-vehicle accident, one injury, male with a head injury. We'll need a medic unit—"*

It sounded like he rolled the volume off, and said, "See what I mean, Angel? It's dangerous out here, tonight." I heard a chirp and he said something over the radio I didn't catch, and said to Angela, "You take care of yourself."

I didn't hear anything else until the door squeaked closed after a few seconds. I put the pry bar away as she came into the bedroom. If she noticed, she didn't mention it, and only beckoned to me and said, "I'm sorry about that."

I kicked my shoes off again and followed her into the living room. "Don't be."

"I am. It's embarrassing." She fell back onto the couch and stared at me, until she said, "Why are you just standing there? Do you want to leave?"

"No."

She patted the spot next to her. "Sit back down, then."

I did. The silence was awkward, and just to say something, I said, "Do people call you that? Angel?"

"No." She looked away and said, "No. I'm Angela. I worked a job where I used that other name. That's where I met him." She took a pull on her beer. "He knows I don't care for it but calls me that anyway. He thinks it's funny. I did too, at first but it got old a long time ago."

"He's a cop."

"Yes. Yes, he is." She stared at the candle flame. "He's an asshole, too."

I touched Angela's shoulder with the back of my fingers. "Hey." She looked up, and I said, "None of us want to be alone. Sometimes we connect with someone handy."

She put her hand on my cheek. "You're sweet, Pete." She smiled, said, "Sweet Pete," and kissed me.

If I got out of this mess, Susan wouldn't need to know about this. If I didn't, nothing I did now would matter. I put my arms around Angela and kissed her back. We kept it up for a minute or so, and then she stood, taking my hand and led me back into her bedroom. "Come on."

This was tricky. To have sex with her would leave me vulnerable if Jimmy came back. She undid the buttons on her shirt. It seemed the storm was getting worse. She shrugged her way out of her shirt, put her arms around me and kissed me again, deeply. Her skin felt smooth under my fingers. Jimmy the cop would likely have his hands full for the next few hours. Her hand trailed down my side and around the front of my pants. She cupped my crotch with her fingers, said, "Mmm," and rolled her tongue around mine.

I gently pushed her back until she sat on the edge of the bed. She giggled as I undid my shirt. She took off her bra, then stood, undid her jeans and slid them down her legs and stepped out of them. I was out of my wet clothes by then and we got onto the bed and grappled with each other until she rolled me onto my back and took me in her mouth. I watched her for a few moments but lay back and did my best to divide my attention.

This was crazy for a lot of reasons. It wasn't just that Angela's pal Jimmy could come back—if any of the guys looking for me knew that bar, that's where they'd look. It was likely the bartender was gone but if not, or if they talked to her, in less than a minute, they'd know where I was. If someone kicked in the door now, I was done. I tried to listen for a tell-tale sound but the only thing I heard was the storm and my own breathing.

I rolled Angela over onto her back and went down on her until she came, and we messed around some more. It took some time for me to be ready and when I was, Angela pulled me on top of her and we were fucking. It felt good, and we kept it up for a while but whether it was my apprehension or that I hadn't been with anyone new for a time or both, it had taken me a while to get started and now, I couldn't finish. Angela must have sensed my distraction but read it as something else. She put her hand on my cheek, said, "Hey, relax. Let's take a break," and kissed me. "This is nice. Sometimes, it can be a little weird, the first time with somebody." She rolled over, got up and fished her cigarettes out of her bag. "I hope you don't mind. I don't usually smoke in the house but it's crazy out." She looked around, said, "I gotta find something to use as an ashtray," and walked out of the room.

I heard her rummaging around the living room. I got up and looked out at the dark street. Rain lashed the window. There was a white quarter-ton pickup truck in the driveway alongside the house that I hadn't noticed. It made me wonder why she said she'd gotten a ride to the bar. I also wondered if it ran.

Angela came back into the bedroom with a flowerpot saucer. "Best I could do," she said, holding it up. "Like I said, I don't like to smoke in here. Anytime I do, the place stinks for a week. What's it look like out there?"

"The same." I stared at her for a moment. She looked good without clothes and was unself-conscious around me but there seemed something odd about her now—something not satisfactorily explained by our intimacy. I said, "I don't think it'll let up anytime soon."

"That's okay. I've got nowhere to go." She came over and kissed me. "How about you?"

"Me neither." I kissed her back.

"Hey, look at me." She took me by the shoulders and squared herself to me. "Are you all right?"

"Sure."

"Look," she said and stopped. She started over. "Look, if you're with somebody, I understand—I mean, I didn't ask and I'm not asking now." She let go of me and turned away. Her voice got smaller. "I think I've been around a little longer than you have, so I know, okay? You're a decent-looking guy. It would be natural—I mean these are unusual—you know, with the storm and you're stuck here—" She stopped, abruptly.

I understood then what I'd seen in her a moment ago. No matter what she'd thought about me before, for her now, this wasn't a totally casual encounter. I didn't know what to tell her about Susan, but said, "Until a few days ago, I thought I was with somebody." I thought more about it and said, "We probably hadn't really been together for a while. We went through the motions. Does that make sense?"

"I think so." She looked at me.

I felt uncomfortable and spoke to fill the silence. "I hope so. I like you and I don't want you to think I'm full of shit—"

She put her hand on my lips, said, "It's all right," and kissed me, and then again, with more vigor. I felt myself becoming aroused. We lay back down and this time it was better, I was more able to relax. She closed her eyes and smiled as we fucked and for a while I forgot about where we were and even who I was. When we finished, she lit the cigarette. Exhaling, she said, "That was really good." She sat up and said, "How about I make us tea?"

I stood. "That sounds nice."

"Gather your clothes and I'll throw them in the dryer. Or I could wash them for you first?"

"No, the dryer's fine. Thanks." I knew that must sound odd. I added, "Like you said, we might lose power." As I said that, I became aware that the storm had changed quality, likely some time ago. Instead of gusting, as it had been while I was out of doors, the wind now sounded a deep, steady roar.

"Right. Good thinking." From a chair, she took a sweatshirt that had Stockton University silkscreened across its front and tugged it over her head. She dug through a drawer, said, "I've got—here, I think these will fit you," tossed sweatpants to me and left the room with my wet clothes.

While I tugged on the sweats, I thought about Susan, and what I'd said about her to both Angela and earlier, to the AA people in the church. All of it was true and accurate, but I'd left out my thoughtlessness. This—my life—wasn't normal and I'd accepted that. Expecting Susan or any other straight person to be okay with it indefinitely was ludicrous and unfair.

Angela was making small noises in the kitchen that I heard over the storm—filling the kettle and putting it on the stove. I walked out and watched her take mugs from the cupboard. The hem of her sweatshirt rode up, exposing her ass. I probably shouldn't have offered Susan a ride to the airport in the morning. I doubted there would be any point. I couldn't promise her anything like being a different person or living a different life.

Angela put tea bags in the mugs and turned. She met my gaze and smiled. I thought about what my life alone would be like, at least in the short term and realized I couldn't see anything. Angela came over and kissed me.

I held Angela but as I kissed her back, I realized the sense of loss I felt surrounding Susan had clouded my thinking again, as it had ever since we'd spoken in the car on Wednesday night. If she was truly breaking things off because I'd shown her something in herself that she didn't like, I supposed that was understandable and okay. A crisis of conscience would be different. If she followed that, it might not end until she talked to someone. I couldn't let that happen. I had to talk to Susan before she left, just to get a sense of where her head was.

Angela gasped and stiffened, and then something cold touched my toes. I looked down. A thin layer of seawater was encircling my feet and had already covered much of the linoleum.

Angela said, "Oh, shit."

I let her go. Water was coming through the gap under the backdoor and had already spread under the refrigerator on one side of the room and the cabinets and stove on the other. I turned and watched as the water's leading edge reached the hallway carpet, slowly darkening its nap.

CHAPTER SEVENTEEN

Angela grabbed a kitchen towel hung over the stove door handle and knelt, trying to wedge it into the gap under the back door. "Oh, fuck, fuck, fuck." She turned and said, "Grab some towels from the bathroom." She hopped up and grabbed more towels from a cabinet drawer. "Come on."

At the front door, water had come over the threshold onto the entryway. I said, "Angela, a better strategy would be to get your important things up off the floor." She turned around to speak but I said, "Trust me, water's going to find its way inside, one way or the other."

"It'll wreck the floors, though, won't it?"

"It might. Is your house paid off?"

"No, but what's—"

"It means you have Federal Flood Insurance that will cover this. Don't worry. I've seen what insurance can do, okay?"

She looked unconvinced but said, "Okay," and stood.

I said, "Let's get your important things off the floor."

She nodded, but instead of acting, she began to weep. I put my arms around her and said, "It's going to be all right, Angela. This is all just stuff. You're going to be fine."

"I know, I know. I'm sorry, I know I'm a mess." She rested the side of her head on my shoulder.

"No, you're not."

"I am, though. I work for an asshole at a stupid job. I drink too much." She sobbed, shaking in my arms and said, more quietly, "And, as you've seen tonight, I'm a booty-call for a married guy who doesn't really like me." She wiped at her nose with the back of her hand. "You must think I'm a real loser."

"I don't think that at all." I held her and said, "You're a bright, talented person who is muddling through, the best you can, like most of us are. I think you've chosen a nice path to muddle along."

"Thanks. You're sweet." She looked around the kitchen but didn't move. "I've felt like a loser all my life. I started at Saint Rita's in the third grade. We moved to Philadelphia from Pittsburgh. I don't know about Trenton, but in Philadelphia, if you weren't born there, you're always the new kid."

I watched the water rolling in under the door but said, "Trust me, it's the same everywhere."

She spoke as though I hadn't said anything. "I went to Girl's High. By then, I'd grown tits and I was pretty enough to hang out with the other pretty girls, but I always felt like I didn't belong with them. Like, if I said or did the wrong thing, they'd drop me."

I spoke softly. "That's the difference between a bunch of friends and a clique."

"What's that?"

"Friends are easy with each other. Everyone in a clique feels at risk, all the time."

"Really? It wasn't just me?"

"Think about it. You know I'm right." I needed to get her back to practical thinking. It wouldn't help either of us if her house floated away. I looked at her stove. It was electric. I said, "Do you have a gas furnace or water heater?"

She looked puzzled for a moment but got it and said, "No, no, everything is electric."

"Good. We don't have to worry about rising water putting out pilot lights."

"Do you think it will get that bad?"

"It might. Better to think ahead. Why don't we take down your pictures and put them in plastic bags?"

She nodded. "That's a good idea. I'm glad you're here. I'm sorry I started freaking out."

"You're okay. Let's do that and get things up off the floor."

There wasn't much. The main thing she wanted to keep dry was the bureau in her bedroom. "It was my grandmother's. It's probably not expensive but I'm—I'd rather it didn't get wrecked."

"It's very nice. The easiest thing would be to put it up on the bed."

"My couch is big, but we might have a tough time, both of us trying to sleep on it."

"Your bureau won't fit on the couch." I said, "It's probably best we don't try to sleep, at least for a while." I pulled the shade away from the window but couldn't see much. "Have you ever seen it this bad?"

"No. I mean, it was at least this bad during Sandy, but I wasn't here for it. I was in Philadelphia for my girlfriend's wedding, and I stayed up there for a few days after. I didn't have this house then but you're right, insurance took care of the things in my apartment—new carpet and stuff."

My backpack was in front of the bottom drawer, and she tugged it out of the way by one handle. "Christ, what's in that, rocks?" She reached inside and pulled out my hat. "I'll hang this up for you," and hooked it onto a peg in the closet.

We lay the bureau on its back across the bedspread. She had a dozen pairs of shoes on the floor of her closet and put them up, too. I put my backpack on the foot of the bed.

In the living room, I said, "Your couch is going to get wrecked unless you have something we can put under the legs to prop it up."

"It's okay, I trash-picked it."

"Really? It's in decent shape."

"Yeah, that's why I took it. I was coming back from the bar one night in my little truck and saw it out on the curb. A guy helped me. It wasn't until we got it inside here that I saw the note on the arm that read "Salvation Army Pickup."

I chuckled. "No sense in taking it back after all the work you did, moving it."

"Oh, hell no." She laughed. "I'm getting another beer. Want anything?"

"No thanks."

The water on the floor was two inches deep now. I heard a tearing sound above. Angela said, "Jesus. What the hell was that?"

"I think you just lost some of your roof."

"Great." She came back into the living room. "The floors are fucked and now I'll lose my ceilings, too."

"No, you won't. Once we see water on this side, I'll use my awl to put a hole in the low point. Most of the water will come through that. You'll be okay."

She smiled. "You are one handy mofo to have around." She kissed me. "I want you to know that you have an open invitation here." She kissed me again. "Anytime you want."

"Thanks, Angela. I'd like that."

"Let's relax a little." We sat on the couch. She splashed the water on the floor with her bare foot, twice and said, "I always wanted a house with a pool." We chuckled.

On the television were live shots of the storm lashing various locations, mostly along the coast. Angela picked up the remote and said, "Do you mind if we hear what they're saying?"

"Not at all."

She thumbed up the volume. "—has been upgraded. There have been scattered reports of rescues by police and other first-responders of motorists stranded in their cars. People are advised to remain in their homes—"

The audio portion of the transmission broke up for a few seconds, the pictures of the storm still on the screen. The newscaster came back on while footage of Bluff and his remaining crew of state cops played. "In other news, the burglary of a local politician's home early this evening seems to have precipitated a rash of criminal activity, some of which has resulted in at least four deaths. A ranking state policeman has been accused of actions that are questionable."

The shot changed to what looked like a county building. Bluff and his crew were visible. A reporter got in front of them and said, "Officers, County Executive Picozzi claims you entered his home illegally. Would you care to comment?"

One, a big guy, pushed his way past the reporter. Bluff stopped and said, "Yes, I'd be happy to comment. A local policeman who witnessed someone moving inside Mister Picozzi's dwelling called for assistance. My team and I were in the vicinity and monitoring local police radio. We responded. All of this is normal procedure, even under normal conditions. Mister Picozzi has conveniently ignored the fact that tonight, we have anything but normal conditions and local departments are stretched thin. He's ignored that the perpetrator of the break-in assaulted another local policeman, who is currently hospitalized, fighting for his life. This same assailant may also be responsible for the deaths of four state troopers in my command. Mister Picozzi seems unconcerned. As sad as this is, it's typical of the man and his behavior never surprises me." He walked on.

The news anchor came back. "The burglary of the County Executive's home occurred earlier this evening, at dusk. The officer injured in the ensuing altercation with the alleged perpetrator is reported to be in guarded but stable condition in Atlantic City Medical Center. Later in the evening, this same individual is believed to have started a fire in the Bayshore Hotel.

On-screen were five seconds worth of spliced footage—me, coming out of the hotel linen closet, walking toward the camera and another of me going down steps in the fire tower—played in a loop four times. My face was obscured by the brim of my ball cap but there was more than enough there for someone looking carefully to pick me out. As the video ran the announcer was saying, "Security camera footage shows the alleged perpetrator of the fire. Again, this is believed to be the same individual responsible for the break-in at Mister Picozzi's house."

I felt Angela start and draw away from me. Neither of us looked at the other.

CHAPTER EIGHTEEN

There was no point in trying to bullshit her. I said, "There's three-thousand dollars in a brown paper envelope inside my backpack." If she could handle this, good. "I'll give it to you if you let me stay until I can leave safely." If she couldn't, I'd have to tie her up and put her in the closet.

She tugged the hem of her sweatshirt down, to cover herself. "Did you really hurt that man? The cop?"

"No. I'm a professional. The last thing I ever want to do is hurt someone." She was trying to get used to this. I helped her. "That cop chased me around a house and ran headfirst into an outdoor stairway." She'd be able to visualize that easily enough.

"You're," she pointed at the television and said, "you broke into Charlie's home."

"Picozzi is not a good person." I put my hands up and stood. "I'd like to show you something. Come on." She followed me into the bedroom. The water in the house had risen to my ankles. I held open my backpack, let her see the envelope and handed it to her. "Take the cash but look at the cards and passport."

She took the envelope and then stepped backward, away from me, pulled the cards and paged through the passport. "It's Charlie, but—"

"It's a different name."

She was having trouble. I helped her with it. The truth would work, here. "Picozzi is a crook. I don't know much about him but it's likely he's into a lot of things. You probably know that already if you used to work for him. I found that envelope behind a painting near his front door. It's his run-out stash. In case he ever gets the phone call."

Angela was intelligent and she was beginning to understand. Before she got to the next step, I said, "I don't take from citizens, regular people, okay?" That was a lie, but she didn't know that, and it might make her feel more at ease. I kept going. "I really do have a straight job."

"Then, why do you do this?"

That was what Susan had wanted to know but the answers I'd given her had worn out over time and become unconvincing. They could still work now, with Angela. I said, "I can't pay off my student loans with what I make at my job."

It worked. "I couldn't, either." She nodded and said, "For a while, I danced at a club in Atlantic City. That's where I worked for Charlie."

"You know what I mean, then."

"Yeah. We do what we have to." She took a sip of her beer. "It took me years to pay mine. If I'd known—" She let that hang and was quiet for a few moments and said, "Honest? You don't hurt people?"

"No. That's foolish. The police look a lot harder for you if you've hurt someone." She needed more. I held out my backpack. "Take a look. There's no gun in there, no weapon, only tools."

She ignored that and said, "What about the fire in the hotel?"

"That was a tiny fire I set in a broom closet. I needed to set off the alarm so I could get away."

She nodded but stayed on her side of the couch. She said, "This is going to take a little getting used to."

"I know and I apologize for the way I approached you." I let that sit a moment and said, "I'm glad I did, though."

"You didn't approach me." Despite herself, she chuckled. "I knew I was going to fuck you when you walked into the bar." She reached out for my hand and pulled me toward her. "I got tired of waiting for you to say something to me, so I asked you about health insurance."

"I remember."

"Keep your money. You've been through enough, tonight."

An explosion sounded, at a distance. A moment later, the lights went out along with the television, and the dryer stopped running. I supposed that this time, a transformer really blew. Angela said, "Well, that's that." She picked up the candle on her coffee table, got up and moved toward the hall. "I've got some more in the kitchen."

I was adjusting to the dark, and a small movement caught my eye—the clock's second hand. I heard a drawer open and her rummaging around inside it. She came back into the living room with two more candles and a saucer.

She sat and lit the candles one at a time, anchoring them to the saucer with melted wax.

A question occurred to me. "Angela, do you know if Picozzi is a gambler?"

"I doubt it. He never mentioned it, if he was, and he'd always talk to us when he came by the club. Never hitting on us, just being nice and funny. He'd say, 'Do those degenerates out there have anything left to tip you with, girls?' One of us would usually say something like, 'No, Charlie. You need to give us all a raise.' He isn't a bad guy, but he never had anything nice to say about gamblers."

She pointed with her thumb, over her shoulder toward the street outside and said, "That's where I met *him*—Jimmy, the guy who came over earlier. He worked the door at the club. Charlie liked having off-duty cops for that, and Jimmy was there until he got fired for putting a customer in the hospital. He used to be nicer to me. We kept in touch. I don't really know why." She was quiet for a while. "I quit as soon as I had things with my money under control. Not many people I see around here even know I danced, and most of the ones that do are friends." She was quiet for a while, staring at the candle flame. "I've never felt ashamed or anything, it's just a part of my life that's over."

"I understand." This was an opportunity to make her feel better about me. I said, "I hope to put all this behind me, too, some day."

"You will, if that's what you want."

I sat with that for a few moments. I'd been lying to her but maybe it was the thing to do. I'd had bad luck. And been careless. Mostly, I'd been careless. I'd been thinking about Susan instead of preparing for the job.

Angela must have seen something in my face that scared her. She looked alarmed and blurted out, "Jimmy will help you, if I ask him. He'll do it for me, I know he would."

I hadn't expected that. "Angela, if you want me to go, I will. You don't have to play me." If she didn't want me to stay, my leaving would still be out of the question. I'd never survive outdoors in this storm.

"No, no, this isn't a trick. I mean it sincerely. I don't think you'll be able to get out of town on your own and I don't want—" she choked off the rest and began to cry.

I spoke as softly as I could and still be heard. "I'll get out of this town as soon as the storm's over. I'm good at this work, I've just had bad luck tonight." In the extreme, I'd have to tie her up and lock her in her bedroom. I didn't want to do it. "Please, don't think about calling Jimmy."

"I won't." She looked down and said, "It was a bad idea. I won't think about it anymore."

The wind had sounded a constant howl for a long while. Now, there came a higher-pitched *crack* from the backyard, and what felt and sounded like a truck had run into the back of the house, along with the sound of breaking glass. A blast of wind blew out the candles. We got up and slogged through the calf-deep water. The house shook with a constant but arhythmic thudding.

Moment by moment, I could feel the air pressure changing inside the house, like it was breathing in and out.

Rain hit my face as I came into the darkened kitchen, and I could make out that the tree outside had come down and broken the window above the sink. It was hitting the back of the house, either as the wind gusted or flood water currents shifted, or both. Angela said, "Oh, no. This is fucked." She stared and said, "My poor tree."

An open window could be catastrophic. Houses have blown to pieces in these conditions. I said, "I'm going to take a look," and held the back door against the wind as I eased it open. I was instantly soaked again. Even if we survived the collapse, we wouldn't last long without shelter. As I pushed open the storm door, the wind blew it out of my hand. The screws holding fast the closer were torn from the jamb and the door swung all the way open, slamming into the back wall of the house.

I stepped down into the flooded backyard, keeping a hand on the railing. Angela's magnolia tree had snapped and blown over, into the house, still fixed to the earth at its stump but rocking with the tide. Along with breaking the window, it had shattered some of the siding tiles. I knew there was no point but kept my hand on the wall, waded to the broken tree and pushed. It was too heavy to move away from the house. Turning away, I was blown over as the wind gusted. I came out of the water, sputtering and crawled to the back steps. I'd thought it was bad earlier, but this was beyond anything I had imagined. I got back inside the house and forced the door shut.

I got up and knelt on the counter and began to pull shards of glass away from the frame, squinting against the rain and wind. Angela said, "Is there anything I can do?"

I stopped and said, "Yes, do you have a pair of gloves?"

"Work gloves? Yeah, I have some I garden in." She went through the drawer and handed me a pair in brown cotton. I tugged them on and finished clearing away the broken glass. Rain whipped my face all the while.

Angela said, "Now what?"

I came off the countertop and said, "Now we find something to cover the hole with. Is there a board under your mattress?"

"No, it's just the box spring on slats."

I looked up at the ceiling. "How about your attic? Is there flooring or are there bare ceiling joists?"

"Yeah, there is floor in one area, but I have a ton of crap up there."

"Okay." I looked at her kitchen table. "We'll leave the floorboards alone for the time being. Do you have any hardware? Nails or screws?"

"Yeah, I have a bunch." She rummaged through her junk drawer again, picking out nails. As she looked, I cleared the salt and pepper shakers from the table and turned it on its side. The Formica top covered plywood, dark brown, now, with age.

She saw what I was doing. "Do you have to nail through my table?"

"I'm afraid so." I turned it around and pushed it to the sink cabinet. "The wind will blow it away if I don't. I'll take it easy. Let me see what you've got." I held my hand out. "Can you get me a pencil, too?"

She handed me about a dozen ten penny nails and three sixes. Screws would have held better, but I didn't have a drill and besides, there was no power. I would work with what I had. I tapped the wall in places around the window frame with my hatchet. It felt like I'd get good nailing.

She came back and gave me a pencil. I marked the ceiling above the window opening's borders, and said, "Okay, help me get this into place."

We hoisted the table on end, fighting the wind coming through the window, over the spigot and set it to rest on the back edge of the countertop. Its legs, still attached, projected over the sink, into the room. While Angela held it against the wind, I sighted down my pencil marks and drove nails through the table's underside and into the frame around the window. In a few minutes, I had it secure, and grabbed one of its legs and shook; it held. "This should be okay."

I collected my tools. Sloshing through the hallway to the bedroom, I realized I was exhausted. I put the bag back on the bed next to the grandmother's bureau and made my way to the couch in the living room, grabbed my jacket and sat. "Angela, tonight has been more than I'd counted on. Do you mind if we stretch out? If I fall asleep, I won't snore. I promise."

She said, "You go right ahead. I'm going to catch another smoke, out in the kitchen. I'll be back in a little bit. I'll bring us a dry blanket."

I pulled my jacket around me. I saw her aluminum softball bat, took it to the couch with me and lay down. Angela waded through the shallow water, down her hallway. I closed my eyes.

I only dozed, staying in that space between sleep and wakefulness. From time to time, I would slip below the layer and realize that my conscious thoughts had become fantastic, and I'd come back awake. I needed real sleep, but this helped a little. There was no telling what conditions outside would be like a few hours from now so there was little point in speculating. I thought I heard Angela talking to herself in the kitchen but reasoned it was my imagination. After a while, she lay down with me.

I sensed the storm was lessening. From time to time, I heard what must have been outboard motors, likely police or firemen, helping where they could. I relaxed more as the night caught up with me and wondered if I could get out of town in time to see Susan at the airport like I'd told her. If not, she'd add that to her list of complaints. I could almost hear her, talking about my new undependability.

CHAPTER NINETEEN

I came wide awake as something pressed against my eye. I opened the other and looked along a pistol barrel, ending at fingers curled around its grip. Jimmy said, "Don't you fucking move."

"Take it easy," I said. "I'm not moving."

Angela said, "It's okay, I got scared and called Jimmy. Don't worry, he's going to drive you out of town." She was out of my limited field of vision but sounded like she was standing in front of her television. She sounded nervous.

"That's right. I'll take you to the bus terminal in Atlantic City. Now, real slow, I want you to give me your arm." I did, and he snapped a cuff around my wrist. "Good boy. Now, I want you to roll over toward the back of the couch, onto your stomach."

Angela said, "What are you doing, Jimmy?"

"I'm here to collect your playmate." He looked at me and smiled, but said to her, "Like you asked me to."

"But you promised me you'd give him a ride out of town."

"I will, Angel. I just need to make sure he doesn't try to jump me." He took the pistol away from my face and motioned at me with it. "Go on, now, Tiger. Roll over, like I said."

"He's not going to take me out of town, Angela."

He used his cop voice. *"Roll over. Now."*

When I did, he stuck the muzzle against the back of my neck. I said, "He isn't taking me to jail, either."

He said, "Shut up," grabbed the loose cuff, pulled my free arm behind me. In one deft move he had me cuffed behind my back.

"I'm sorry, Angel, I need to take this one in. He's broken about two dozen laws tonight. I'll bet he's wanted other places, too."

"He's taking me to a dirty cop who's going to kill me."

"He's going to jail, Angel."

Angela was beginning to get it. She said, "Then why are you all alone? Why don't you have help?"

"Oh, I was pretty sure I could handle this one all by myself."

I said, "A second ago, he was worried about me jumping him—"

"*I told you to shut up.*" He pushed the mouth of his pistol against my neck and said to Angela, "Guys like him will say anything." He calmed himself, and said, "Huh. I knew you were busy with someone tonight. Shit-for-brains that I am, I figured you were bunked up with one of the nail-bangers you know from the supply house."

"Don't talk to me like that."

Jimmy chuckled and said, "Come on, Angel. You know I'm just kidding around."

I said, "Jimmy kids around a lot, doesn't he?"

He grabbed the cuff chain and pulled my arms back and up, dragging me off the couch. It was an old-school cop move. I fell into the water on the floor. Before I could turn and sit up, he put his foot on my back, holding my head underwater. While I thrashed, I could hear what sounded like Angela yelling. After a few moments, he came off me and I got myself up, out of the water, sputtering. Jimmy was laughing. I worked my legs under me and was trying to stand when he said, "No, no, pal. I want you right there, on your knees.

Angela said, "Jimmy, you said you wouldn't hurt him."

"Come on, he isn't hurt." He said to me, "Are you?" He reached into his pocket, took out a cell phone and pushed a button. "Son of a gun." Still smiling, he turned the phone to us. Its face was lit. "It still works." He thumbed a text message and sent it.

I was still coughing, but said, "How about letting me sit on the couch? My knees are getting sore."

"You'll forget about your knees if I shoot you."

Angela said, "Stop it, Jimmy."

"Relax, Angel." He stared at me and said, "*Walt* knows I'm just messing around. Right, *Walt?*" To Angela, he said, "Earlier tonight, your playmate here told me his name was Walt. What did he tell you?"

I said, "Hey, Angela, ask him what he's waiting for." She looked at me, confused. "He could make a call, if he wanted help or just take me in, right now, by himself. I'm cuffed, I can't do much. What's he waiting for?"

Jimmy said, "That's enough out of you."

Angela said, "I think that's a question you should answer, Jim."

I said, "I can tell you." To Jimmy, I said, "You're waiting to hear from Bluff. Him or one of his friends, like Lloyd or Robby, right?"

"Oh, you know some names."

Angela said, "What's going on, Jimmy? Who are those people?"

"Cops, Angel. Just cops."

"State cops, right, Jim? Nobody you work with."

Something in Jimmy's face changed. I'd pushed it too far. I needed to keep him talking before he decided to simplify things. I said, "What's with him and Picozzi?"

"Why you want to know?"

"For my own edification." He stayed silent. I said, "It means I'd just like to know."

"Fuck you. I know what it means."

"Come on, then." I shook the cuffs behind me. "You got me. What's up with them."

He was quiet for a moment, and said, "Bluff wrote him up for speeding." Jimmy smiled. He was enjoying himself again, so

I let him take his time. "Bluff was just going to give him a warning, but Picozzi gave him a ration of shit for stopping him. Buff wrote him up and then walked around the car and cited him for anything he could. Picozzi already had a lot of drag, so he got out of it all, but it's been war between them ever since. A few months ago, Bluff was up for the number two spot with the staties, and Picozzi made sure he got passed over. Tonight, Bluff was trying to return the favor. I'm not sure what his plan was but it all fell apart once you fucked up that kid."

Angela had stayed quiet but said, "You told me he hit his head on outdoor stairs?"

"Now, that's a good one." Jimmy chuckled and said, "What else did he tell you, Angel?"

I faced Angela and said, "That's what happened."

Jimmy said, "He's put at least half a dozen guys in the hospital tonight. Killed a few, too." He faced me and said, "You're just one bad motherfucker, aren't you?"

I needed to keep Angela on my side. "None of that answers what he's waiting for."

I had her. She said, "Answer the question, Jim. What's going to happen?"

Jimmy didn't say anything.

I said, "Like a lot of people, Jimmy knows about Picozzi's twenty-thousand-dollar reward to bring me in. I don't think twenty is enough for Jimmy. He knows there's a better offer." I turned to Angela. "That guy Bluff will pay Jimmy a lot more to keep things quiet." I faced Jimmy again. "Am I close?"

He stayed mute.

"Think about it, Angela. Picozzi will be happy to give Jimmy his money to put me in the hot seat and see if I'll say who set up the break-in."

Jimmy said, "I could probably tell Picozzi who that is myself."

"No. You couldn't play in his league. That guy would snuff you out like a candle flame." Jimmy didn't like that. I kept going.

"Your bosses will want to know how you let me get away earlier tonight. I didn't see any cameras at the police station, but Mona could tell them about me. Gonna kill her, too, Jim?"

"I'm not too worried about her."

I looked at Angela. "His bosses will wonder how he knew I was here."

"Ha. Police work. That's how I knew."

I ignored that and said, "Jimmy's wife is going to be curious about that, too." I let Angela think about that for a moment and said, "If I was to just disappear, none of those inconvenient questions will come up."

Jimmy said, "Angela, you know that's not me." He kept his eyes on me as he spoke. "If I was going to kill this guy, why haven't I already? What's stopping me?"

"Easy," I said. "They'll stiff you. Bluff and his crew are ranking state cops. Investigators. You're a flatfoot in a two-bit shore town. You're nobody." I was pushing it but saw that Angela was understanding. I pushed a little harder. "You throw his nickname around like you're both great pals, but I bet he doesn't even know who you are."

Jimmy made to say something but stopped.

I kept it up. "They left you at Picozzi's house to hold the scene." I spoke to Angela but kept him in sight. "That's the kind of job good cops give to zeros."

Jimmy laughed and said, "Fuck you." He'd tried to keep his affect amused but I'd irked him.

I turned to Angela. "If he shoots me now, he's got nothing." She was smart but this had been a long night and we'd taken her out of her world with all this. I helped her. "If I'm already dead, that state cop's problems are over. He won't give Jimmy a cent, and there's nothing Jimmy could do about it."

Jimmy turned to her now and said, "Angel, sorry—Angela, I'm waiting for back-up. You've seen how dangerous this guy is. I'll bring him in and split the reward with Larry."

"Then show her that last text you sent." I said to Angela, "I bet he didn't send it to Larry."

I saw in her face that she understood. Jimmy did, too, but he kept trying. "Ten-thou is a nice chunk of change." He was trying to think of something to say that might sound convincing or at least comforting. "We could go somewhere nice, you and me." He was running down. "A vacation. What do you think? Nasau?"

I said, "The thing is, Angela, once I disappear, you'll have to go, too." It looked like she was already ahead of me, but I kept it up. "Nothing's going to be enough to buy you and he knows it." She put her hand on her potted cactus. "He's going to kill you, too."

Jimmy said, "Shut up."

I kept it up. "He'll drown you, right here in your house, put you outside and let you float away. You'll just be another storm victim."

Jimmy came at me with his gun hand raised. *"Shut the fuck up!"*

Angela slung the flowerpot into the back of his head. He staggered and went unfocused for a moment but turned and hit her. She fell back into the water as I got my feet under me and drove my shoulder into his middle, just below his belt. I couldn't generate much power but felt the wind go out of him. He fell onto the beanbag chair. It burst open at a seam, spilling its tiny plastic beads into the flooded room.

I toppled and fell, rolled onto my back, rocked backwards, my head underwater, brought my knees to my chest and swung my cuffed hands up, past my feet and in front of me, like I was skipping rope backwards. I'd seen another guy do this a few months before, and had practiced the move, since.

Jimmy was trying to move quickly but was a moment slow getting up, and I got a hand on his gun and held it away from me as we grappled. He was strong. I got my other hand on his wrist, below the pistol and tried to wrench it out of his hand. Angela

jumped on his back and raked at his eyes with her nails, screaming all the while. Jimmy pounded me with his free hand. He fired
twice, pointlessly, and the rounds went into the ruined beanbag.

I held on but he twisted his leg around mine, flipped me onto
my back and held my head under. I gagged on a mouthful of
salt water as I floundered. He outweighed me by at least forty
pounds. I couldn't budge him but I couldn't let go of his gun
hand, either. I was vaguely aware of Angela's voice, her screaming audible through the water, and I was just able to bring one
knee up and bridge, upsetting him enough to twist away and
up. I gasped a breath as I broke the surface, choking. He kept
punching the back of my neck and trying to force my head back
under. I heard a hollow thump and he grunted and stopped.
Then another, louder cracking sound and he loosened his grip. I
flipped him onto his back, and pinned him there, his face underwater, my shoulder in his throat. Angela dropped the softball bat
in the water and just stood there, crying. Jimmy was struggling,
ferociously, and I almost lost my purchase. I shouted to Angela,
"He'll kill us both if you don't help me." She sat on his legs, crying, loudly now. Jimmy was shaking but ran down quickly. He
might have aspirated salt water. Angela must have done real
damage when she hit him. He stopped moving and went limp.
Angela sobbed, the entire time.

Victims of asphyxiation have auto-recovered, even after six
or seven minutes. I held him there while I watched Angela's clock.

CHAPTER TWENTY

I'd only counted two minutes and forty-two seconds, when Angela said, "Get off him." I stayed where I was and kept my eyes on the clock.

"*I said, get off him.*" I looked. She had Jimmy's gun, not pointing it at anything, just holding it. "Is he dead?"

As gently as I could, I said, "He meant to kill us both, Angela." This was bad for lots of reasons. I didn't want to deal with a body, least of all, a dead cop. First, I had to get Angela's head around this, for her own good. I stood slowly and said, "You know that don't you?"

"*No.*" She was still trying to tell herself that none of this had happened. I waited, and she said, "No. He was my friend." Jimmy had split her lip when he hit her. I took a step, but she wasn't ready. She brought the pistol up, pointed toward me, said, "Stay where you are," and licked away blood.

"Easy." I stopped and held up my cuffed hands, palms forward. I wouldn't reach her in time if I tried to rush her. I didn't want to do that, anyway, if I didn't have to. She was smart. I tried to lay it out. "If you call the police and hold me here, they won't believe that you couldn't have done anything." I nodded toward the pistol in her hand. "If you shoot me first, they're still going to want to know why he drowned." She was thinking. I added. "If you shoot him, too, the autopsy will show he was shot after he was already dead. Any way you try to play this by punishing me, there's going to be too many questions. You're not going to talk your way out of trouble." I let her realize I was right and said, "Let me handle this and I can make it go away. You'll be safe."

"You'll kill me for calling him."

"No. You were frightened and made a mistake." She didn't look convinced. I said, "I'll have nothing to fear from you if you're alive and well. If you were either found dead or went missing, the police will have more reason to look for me than they already do."

She was smart. I was sure that she understood the practical side of everything I'd told her. The tough part would be the emotional aspect. I said, "I heard how he spoke to you when he didn't get his way, tonight. I'll bet it wasn't the first time, either." Before she could say anything else, I said, "I'm sure he could be nice, and was fun sometimes, but friends don't do that to each other."

She didn't say anything, but her sobbing had stopped.

I spoke more quietly. "Angela, how often did he call you by that other name?"

She looked away. After a moment she nodded her head. "You're right." She looked back at me, then. "What—what do we do—"

I put my hand on her arm. She gave a start but let me slide my hand down to hers and take the pistol from her fingers. I turned her away and said, "I'll take care of it," found Jimmy's keys, undid the cuffs and put them and the keys in my pocket. I moved her, gently, toward the hallway, through the beads floating in the dirty water to the kitchen and had her sit on the countertop. I put my arm around her. "It's going to be all right."

After a moment, she said, "Your name's not Pete, is it?"

"No but why don't you call me that, anyway?"

I felt her nod. "You're not from Trenton, either."

"No."

"So, I was just a way out of the storm."

It was a statement, not a question, but I answered her. "Back there, at the bar, yes. I didn't know anything about you besides you looked good. Be honest, that's all I was to you, too." I felt her nod. "Talking with you tonight, seeing your art, it makes it different. I know you better. Does that make sense?"

"I don't know."

"Do you believe me?"

"I want to."

"Can that be enough for now?"

She nodded again but said, "What should we do—"

"Stay here. Give me a few minutes."

I got my street clothes out of her dryer. They were still wet. I shook my way out of her sweatpants and pulled my clothes and my shoes on and slogged back through the hallway. Jimmy was where I'd left him. An arm rocked gently with the movement of the water in the little house, along with the hundreds of tiny plastic beads.

It took some trouble to get his first arm through and out of the sleeve of his slicker. The other slid off. Jimmy's wallet was in his front pants pocket and came away easily enough. In it were his badge and ID. I didn't look anything like him, but it could work at a distance if I needed it to. He had about thirty dollars. His uniform hat had come off and was underwater, and I had a little trouble finding it. It, and the raincoat were too large for me, but not enough to matter.

I dragged Jimmy through the water to the front door. I didn't like taking him outside, but I couldn't leave him in the house. Angela was beyond upset. If she saw Jimmy's corpse in her living room, it could be too much.

I opened the door, looking for movement. Seeing none, I stepped down the front stairs, deeper into the flood water. It seemed safe. The wind and rain had noticeably lessened. It seemed the sky was lighter, now, too. The water was moving but slowly. There was no evidence of anyone nearby, outdoors or in any of the homes I could see.

I went back inside and hooked a cuff around Jimmy's wrist and dragged him out the front door. Around the side of the house, there was space on the far side of Angela's pickup truck, between it and the four-foot storm fence. He'd be out of sight from her windows. I fixed him there with the other cuff.

In the near distance, away from the bay, I could make out a hollow, thumping sound and waded toward it. Jimmy hadn't gotten here by car or on foot. He had to have a boat.

There was a lot of devastation. Most of the homes I saw showed some damage. A few were leveled. In the next block, two utility poles were leaning thirty degrees off vertical, either uprooted or snapped off at the base, only held up by the wires and cables strung between them and other poles still standing. A sixteen-foot Jon boat fitted with an outboard motor was lashed to one nearest me. The currents were bumping it against the pole. I reasoned the power company wouldn't energize the lines until they had restored its infrastructure, but it had me nervous as I slogged toward them through the thigh-high water.

I thought the boat would need bailing out, but a pump, the size of my fist, was humming away, pushing rainwater through a clear plastic tube, out of the boat. A thin cable ran from the little pump to the outboard, and I saw there was an electric ignition system with a battery. It made sense—it would take a strong pull to get an engine this big started manually. Jimmy's radio was there, too.

I undid the leader and towed the boat toward Angela's. I couldn't know who was nearby and didn't want to attract attention by firing up the outboard before I was ready to go. It took some effort, but I made it and lashed the boat to the bumper of her pickup truck.

Jimmy was still floating where I'd left him, held in place against the fence by the current. I undid the cuffs, put them back on his belt and heaved him up, into the boat.

Back in her house, I found Angela wading through the water and plastic beads, pacing, her arms folded in front of her. The water had gone down and was only a few inches deep. I picked up my backpack and said, "Are you going to be all right?"

She nodded, not looking at me. "You know what I said before, about you coming around sometime?" She sounded like it was all catching up to her, and a moment later, answered her own question. "I don't—it would be better if you didn't."

I wasn't surprised and only said, "I'm sorry things happened the way they did, Angela."

She nodded again and I went back outside.

CHAPTER TWENTY ONE

The outboard started with the push of a button, and I pulled on Jimmy's uniform hat, spun us around and headed toward the ocean. The wind was still strong and pushed the boat around. The houses on either side of the street were too low, here, to be much of a buffer. A couple times, Jimmy's hat almost blew away. I wrung out my handkerchief, tied it around my head and put the hat back on. It was snug.

I kept on, past Quinn's. Its sign was gone, ripped away by the storm, along with most of its roofing, but the building stood. Two blocks farther, over the noise of the outboard, I heard someone behind me yell, "Hey. *Hey!*"

I turned and throttled down. It was Rory, the little drunk, who wouldn't give me a ride the night before. He was shirtless and stood thigh-deep in floodwater, in front of a half-collapsed house. I could see sky through its open doorway, behind him. The stake body's front fender was bashed in. Water was level with its wheel wells. "I could use some help over here."

I yelled, "Everybody could," and kept going.

A few blocks farther on, I went down a street that dead-ended at the beach. The water had receded enough that the tops of the dunes were visible. Water drained slowly toward the sea through the flooded footpath. Much of the dune on either side of the approach had washed away, exposing the Geo-Mesh.

I throttled down as I felt the pull of the current. I needed to decide about Jimmy's pistol and wallet. If his body was found, I wanted his death ruled accidental. That would be more likely if he was found with those. I wasn't happy about disarming myself again, but the law looked diligently for cop killers.

I knew where two other weapons were on the island. One was in Rory's truck. I didn't want to go back, and Rory would likely be upset if he saw me. The little prick was liable to have other guns in his home. Another consideration was that if I used that hand cannon, I'd probably go deaf. The other weapon I knew about was in Picozzi's toilet tank.

I muscled Jimmy's head and shoulders up, resting on the top of the boat's side, and inched him farther out until I had enough leverage to heave him overboard. I watched as he slowly drifted with the flow, through the footpath and away. He might never be found. If he was, I hoped he'd be counted among the victims of the storm—just a guy who'd had bad luck. I tossed his radio into the water.

I twisted the throttle and headed north, parallel to the flooded beach, just inside the dunes until Picozzi's house came into view. I throttled down and watched. There was no evidence of anyone being there but that didn't mean much. The power was out on the island, and it didn't look like anyone was home anywhere.

I got out, lashed the boat to one of the next home's footers and waded through the flood water. Picozzi's ground-level door was locked. I climbed the outdoor steps, checking the upstairs doors until I was on the deck.

It felt like a long time had passed since I'd been here, but it had only been twelve hours. I stepped over the rail. The wind had dried off the shakes and I made it to the dormer, pushed open the sash and stepped inside.

I went to the master bath, recovered the Beretta from the tank and dried it with a bath towel. As I took the inside stairs down, I smelled fresh coffee. Picozzi was in his kitchen, one floor above beach level. He was standing with his arms far enough away from his body that I could see his hands were empty. Beyond that, he looked at ease and said, "This is the second time you've broken into my home."

Without thinking, I said, "Why aren't you frightened?"

"I've done you no harm." Picozzi wasn't physically imposing but seemed tough and looked as though nothing had happened last night. He must have showered and changed since he got home from Mays Landing. His curly gray hair had a semblance of a part. He took up a French press from the counter, poured coffee into a mug and tried a sip. It looked like it was too hot. "Why should you want to hurt me?"

"You put Twenty K on my head last night."

"That money kept you alive. That fucking cop put up more to have you killed. I did you a favor."

"It's a lot of money."

"I'd never pay it." He tried another sip and put the cup down. "Anybody giving you up would be dirty. I'd scare the shit out of them."

"So, you are a crook."

"I'm a politician. I do what I have to." He tapped his breast. "I'm having a smoke."

"Go ahead."

He took a gold cigarette case and lighter from his inside jacket pocket, and said, "I don't need your permission."

As he lit up, I said, "I didn't see your car."

"My aide dropped me off and went to check on her house. She's got a four-wheeler. My car wouldn't make it." He blew out a stream of smoke and checked his gold wristwatch. "She'll call when she gets back to pick me up. Probably about ten minutes."

"I met your woman, last night. Nice lady."

"Yes, she is." He took another drag and said, "She said you were nice, too. For a thief."

"Did she turn me up?"

"Nah, I could tell something was going on once she started talking." He smoked and said, "She can't help it."

I stared at him a moment and said, "You could call the police as soon as I leave."

"I could." He gestured toward the beach with his cigarette and said, "I also could have called them when I saw you coming toward my house in your little boat, but I didn't." He drank most of his coffee in one swallow. "If anything, you did me some good. One way or another, that asshole's finished." I waited, and he said, "You tell me who set you up to do this thing and we're square." He took one last drag and dropped the butt, sizzling, into the coffee cup.

"How about I do you one better?"

It took him a few moments, but he got it. "That'll work." He put the cup in the sink.

I said, "Did this thing with you and that cop really start over a parking ticket?"

"He likes that story, but it isn't true. Not the whole truth, anyway. It started a long time before that." He paused and said, "You took my things, downstairs."

It wasn't a question. I said, "I'm keeping the money."

"You're gonna hack my accounts."

"I'm not that kind of thief."

"Sure. I'm putting a lock on them, anyway."

"Go ahead, but I'll destroy your sheet of paper along with the ID cards. They're no good anymore."

"That's all right. I'd never really need them. Just something Hap drummed into me. The guy he took over from ended up in prison."

I nodded and backed toward the stairs.

He pointed at the Beretta. "I looked for that. Where was it?"

"The toilet tank."

"Why?"

"At the time, I didn't want it and I didn't want anyone coming home to have it, either."

"Smart. You want to clean it here?"

"Sure."

"Fuck you. Get the fuck out of my house."

I backed down the stairs and went outside.

CHAPTER TWENTY TWO

I torqued the throttle and headed back through town and south. The boat didn't seem to draw much, but the wind had lessened, and the water was receding. I scraped bottom a few places and twice had to step out of the boat and push it across the pavement over a shallow stretch.

The prop snagged on something and the engine stalled as I traversed a large open area. I broke the outboard over the stern, levering it up by its throttle arm. A length of fourteen wire had coiled around the blades. Bits of lumber floated by as I worked to free the prop. A partial sheet of particle board trailed loose Tyvek sheeting.

I heard an engine and looked up. Two state cops in an airboat came around a corner and toward me. I tugged Jimmy's hat over my eyebrows. One said, "Yo. You Nolan?"

I put a hand on Picozzi's Beretta. "That's me." I wasn't sure it would fire, but I couldn't outrun them in this boat. "How are you guys making out?"

He ignored that and held up his portable. "They been calling for you. We thought you might be gone."

"Lost my radio in the drink, somewhere, a few hours ago. I had to hole up in a house on Ray Avenue while it was real bad." I went back to work freeing the prop. "Since then, I've just been cruising around looking for knuckleheads who thought they could ride it out. Till now." I undid the last bit of wire and held it up.

The guy nodded. "Been that kind of night. I'll tell them you're okay."

"Thanks." They waited until I started the outboard. I let them go by and continued, past the last bunch of homes and into the bay. That encounter had been bad luck. It made it less likely that Jimmy's death would be ruled an accident. There was nothing to do about that, now.

I steered the boat into open water. Without anything to buffer the wind, crossing the inlet was difficult. The boat was pushed around. I figured out that throttling up was the best way to negotiate conditions. The bridge to Atlantic City soared above me as I dumped Picozzi's fake ID cards and list of accounts and stuffed the money in my inside jacket pocket. Soon enough, I was across and steered into a channel.

The wind wasn't as bad here and I picked my way between Atlantic City and the marshes, travelling the waterways past the casinos, following markers for the Inside Thorofare. In a lot of places, water was still covering property. There was enough time for me to get to a town on the mainland, pick up a car, make it back to Philadelphia, and meet Susan at the airport, before her flight left. I was certain. More than enough time.

The frame of reference from the channel was foreign to me. I wasn't sure about my location until I saw the little airfield's control tower breach the horizon. When the Dorset Avenue Bridge was in sight, I kept going until I found a spot to beach the Jon boat. I Frisbeed Jimmy's uniform hat into the channel, pulled the handkerchief off my head and stuck the Beretta into my waistband at the small of my back. I punched a dozen or more holes in the bottom of the hull with my awl and hatchet, then got out and pushed the boat back into the channel where it drifted with the current, until it filled and sunk. I didn't know if it would be visible when the water receded to normal levels, but it was something, and kept me from drawing too straight a line, at least for an hour or so. My awl still had a little of the kid's dried blood on it. I washed it off in the channel.

The destruction here seemed as random as it had been in the town I'd left. I walked through an empty parking lot between a grocery and a bait shop. Both were damaged but standing. The streets were still flooded but passable by car and there was some movement. There weren't a lot of cars parked on the street here, and most that were looked totaled. If Buddy didn't show, I could have a problem.

It was about six blocks to his house. Here and there, a few people were present, mostly looking to see what the storm had done to their homes. A few waved. I waved back and kept going.

As I approached Buddy's block, I wondered if I was letting emotion cloud my judgement, so I went over it again. I couldn't know if Bluff or any of the cops he'd been in business with were still alive, but if they were, then killing Buddy would be a way for them to cut any connection between them and this past night's nonsense. Of course, killing me could do that for them too. Of course, killing me could do that for them too. That could help; he was a connection to me, too. Of course, for the cops, killing me could do that for them, too.

Part of me just wanted to boost a car somewhere and go back to Philadelphia, to the airport to see Susan before she left but then I wouldn't know how things shook down, here. I'd be looking over my shoulder. I needed to finish this, now, if possible. The Charger wasn't anywhere in sight, but I still took pains, approaching as carefully as I could.

Buddy's house came into view. All the shades were drawn. The flowering bushes that had flanked his front door were gone, likely uprooted and washed away by the surge. He hadn't had his windows boarded over and a few were broken. That, and maybe half a dozen missing courses of siding was all the damage I could see.

A pane on the south side of the house was cracked. I carefully worked two long shards free, reached through and unlatched the sash. I took a breath; if he was home, I was dead. I raised the sash and placed the loose pieces of glass on the sill before I pushed the shade out of my way and climbed inside. I crouched there, on the wet carpet under the window and listened to the silence inside the house. Satisfied that I was alone, I stood, between the window and its shade, and did my best to replace the loose slivers of glass, fitting them into the groove of the window frame. As best possible, I needed the house to appear unmolested.

I pulled the Beretta and held it while my eyes adjusted to the dim interior. Buddy's living room wasn't what I'd imagined it would be. I'd expected wall-to-wall carpeting, but there was a black rug with a flower pattern in gold covering hardwood flooring. A tan couch stood along the far wall, with a matching loveseat angled into the near corner of the room. A modern floor lamp stood behind it. Maybe his taste was better than I'd assumed, or a woman had helped decorate the place.

The coffee table seemed more Buddy's style. It was two-pieced, with thick glass tops, each half vaguely teardrop-shaped with rounded points—paisleys—built to stand together with a curving but consistent, four-inch gap between them. The walls were done in vibrant colors—reds and purples.

I walked toward the kitchen and noticed Buddy's jacket on the back of a chair in the corner. Someone behind me said, "Stop and empty your hands." The voice was a man's and sounded calm, almost nonchalant, but was clearly the voice of someone used to having people do what he told them. I dropped the Berretta and held my hands out and open, fingers spread.

He said, "I didn't think you'd make it, but I knew you'd come here if you did."

I improvised. "I live next door. Buddy knew I was coming down today and asked me to check on his house, see if there's any damage." The man was quiet. I said, "He forgot to leave me a key."

"Uh huh. Take a few steps forward." I took four and he said, "Stop where you are and kneel down." I did and he said, "Put your hands behind your head, fingers laced." When I'd done that, I heard him walk toward me, and what sounded like him kicking the Beretta behind him. He pressed the muzzle of his pistol against the back of my neck while he patted me down, ran a hand over my calves and ankles, but it was cursory; he was feeling for weapons and missed the bills in my pockets. He took a few steps back and grunted, quietly, and I assumed he'd stooped to take up the Berretta. "Nice piece. You always check your neighbor's houses with a gun in your hand?"

"Of course not. I saw the broken window and thought there might be someone inside. Looters, you know?" He stayed quiet. "Look, can I get up now? So we can talk to each other like normal people do?"

He was quiet a few moments more and said, "Stand up and walk backwards toward me until I tell you to stop. Keep your hands—"

"Yeah, yeah, where you can see them. Of course. I don't want any trouble."

I stood and moved backwards until he said, "Far enough. Turn around, slowly."

I did. A man I didn't recognize stood there with a gun in each hand, one pointed at me. He said, "You're not what I expected." When I didn't speak, he showed me the Berretta. "This gun of yours says you planned to settle up."

"I came to check Buddy's house for him."

"Uh huh." He slid the Beretta into his jacket pocket. The gun pointed at me didn't move. "When did he ask you to do that?"

"Yesterday afternoon."

"Huh. That must be one hell of a phone you've got." He let me think about that and said, "After Buddy left with you the other day, I let myself in. You guys were gone for a while, but I'm patient. I let him finish his phone call before I shot him."

"Nice of you."

He ignored that and said, "He looked pretty dead to me, so I put him under the house. He's got a trapdoor in his utility closet. We planned to move him last night, but, well, you know, things got busy. I hoped the floodwaters would carry him away.

Save us some trouble but he's still there. We'll have to deal with him tonight." He paused a moment and said, "You ought to have looked under the house, first. Good place to be for someone planning an ambush."

"You weren't there."

"Good point."

"Where were you when I came in?"

"Behind the loveseat. You should have looked there, too."

"I'll remember that for next time."

"Sure, you will."

This wasn't going anywhere. "I'm guessing you're a state cop." He didn't say anything. I said, "Look, if Buddy's dead, there's nothing connecting you or anyone else to this mess. If you were here to kill me, you'd have done it already. It's been a long night. How about we give this up and go home?"

"I want the money you got out of Picozzi's house. Gimme your sack."

So, it was the money rumor that was keeping me alive. He'd expect denials first. "Here, see for yourself. I didn't find any money." I shrugged my way free of the backpack and held it out.

"Lay it on the floor and back up." I did, and he said, "Turn around." I faced the kitchen and heard him unzip the bag and dump my tools.

I looked over my shoulder and said, "There was no money."

"Bullshit." He waved me around and shook his head. "I set this up. Buddy was an asshole, but he knew his business. I told him to get a pro for this job and he said he knew just the guy." He pointed at me. "An ace thief. Told me you'd find anything that was in there."

"Oh, he's right. I would have but there was nothing there." The cop stared at me. I said, "How'd you plan to take it? Bluff and the boys weren't trying too hard to catch me at first."

"They weren't. Not till you fucked up that kid. You shouldn't have done that." I shrugged. He said, "Bluff only wanted to get inside Picozzi's place. He didn't know about the money. I got that roadblock detail set up and ready to go, late yesterday afternoon. Then, fuck me, I get called to come help once it all went to shit. But now, here you are."

I needed to push back a little more. "If there really was money, then why would Buddy tell me Picozzi was a degenerate gambler? The story about Saturday night's blackjack money in his house over Friday night?"

"I came up with that. If Buddy tells you about Picozzi's stash, but says he doesn't know his last name, the story falls apart but if you knew who Picozzi is, then you wouldn't do the job. Bluff wanted a story a professional would find believable. I thought it was pretty good."

"Buddy was chummy with Bluff, too?"

"No."

"Where is Bluff?"

I could see that he didn't like the segue and he was deciding whether or not to answer me. There was something familiar about him as he stood there, silently but I couldn't place him. Something in his face changed. He seemed to relax. He likely figured giving a little might make me more agreeable, easier to handle. Plus, he planned to kill me and remembered that nothing he told me would matter. He said, "Trenton."

"I thought your headquarters was in West Trenton?"

"I'm impressed. Bluff was called to the state capitol. Picozzi is tight with the governor." He scratched the back of his neck. "I told Bluff this was a stupid idea. Picozzi wouldn't keep anything incriminating in his house. Bluff was too pissed to listen. He's done real well for himself but the truth is he's rarely been the smartest man in the room. Any room, anywhere. Where's the money?"

I wondered why this seemingly intelligent man would believe a rumor that only the simplest of Picozzi's constituents took to heart. "How much is he supposed to have?"

"It's at least six figures. Gotta be. Cash."

"How do you know that?"

"Cause Picozzi's been in county politics for nearly fifty years and he's a crook. If he helped himself to ten thousand dollars a year, he'd have half a million and I bet he took more than that."

"He might have pissed it away as soon as he took it."

"Nah, he doesn't go for ice water in the summer. He's so tight he squeaks."

I nodded. There was something off about this guy, but I didn't know what.

His impatience was getting the better of him. While he scratched the back of his neck again, he said, "Moving Buddy tonight is gonna be a pain in the ass. It won't be much worse to move you with him."

"Okay, okay, you made your point. I don't have it with me."

"It's in your car."

"No car. I got here by boat."

He was weary of this conversation. This time, there was a brittleness in his voice when he said, "Where's the money?"

I saw it then. He believed the rumor because he wanted to. Behind the coolness he was showing me, he was scared. This wasn't a guy wanting extra money to play with. He needed it. I didn't know what his problem was, but he probably thought a big pile of money could fix things. Or at least help. I said, "I had to stash it in an empty house." He made to speak but I added, "Don't ask the address. I don't know it and I wouldn't give it to you anyway." I pointed to the floor. "You'd leave me here with Buddy."

He chuckled.

I said, "I know how to get there."

"Okay, let's go. My car's down the street."

"No. I'll drive Buddy's car. You follow me. I'll stop out front, tell you where to look and then I leave."

"Come on, that's just insulting. Anyway, that's my car now." He smiled. "Buddy couldn't sign over the title, so I signed it for him."

"How's that going to look once someone finds Buddy?"

"They won't. Besides, it turns out it wasn't even registered in his name. A guy named Ralph Gibson showed on the paperwork."

"Probably his uncle."

"Probably. Neither of them are gonna need it, anymore. So, how are we going to work this to your satisfaction?"

"How about this—you drive Buddy's car—"

"My car."

"Sorry, my error. You drive your car, I'll ride shotgun. We get there, you cuff me to the wheel. You come out with the money, uncuff me and I go away."

He was working it out to take the money and kill me, too. "That leaves you without a ride." He didn't want to seem too eager, so he pretended to be helpful. "How will you get home?"

"I'll manage."

He stayed quiet, as though to mull things over and said, "Okay, come on." He reached behind him and brought out a set of cuffs. "Turn around." He spun his index finger, drawing circles in the air.

"No. That's not going to work." Before he said anything, I added, "I'll walk ahead of you, ten feet or so. If I try anything, you can shoot me. If I'm cuffed, I'll attract too much attention."

"There's nobody on the street."

"There are and there's only going to be more, the later it gets."

He thought about it for a long moment. "I still gotta cuff you. You'll wear the bracelets up front. Back into the wall." I did. He moved around me and grabbed Buddy's leather jacket from the chair. "We'll cover them with this." I stayed where I was. He said, "Let's go. Hands," and beckoned with his fingers.

I'd be cuffed in the car during the ride through Atlantic City and over the bridge. I still had Jimmy Nolan's handcuff key. It would likely work for these, too. If not, I'd think of something else. I put my hands out, together. He snapped them on and draped the jacket over my hands. "Don't forget I've got the pistol."

He put it in his jacket pocket and kept his hand there. I bent to collect my tools, but he said, "You can come back for them."

I thought it better not to argue. I walked to the front door and grasped the knob two-handed. There was a hole in Buddy's jacket, in its back. The cop said, "Don't get cute, let's go. Leave the door open behind you."

I stepped down to the walkway. He shut the door and said, "Go on. Take a right."

I did, and said, "So who are you, Robby or Lloyd?"

He didn't answer for a few moments. "They got blown up." Before I could ask a follow up, he said, "Let's not worry about names. I don't want to know yours."

"Fair enough." Outside now, in the light, I recognized him. He was the guy who'd held the shotgun, that one time I'd brought Buddy items to move.

We walked a block and turned inland. He kept me to the street side of the pavement, to keep his free hand on the back of my arm. Knowing where I'd seen this guy didn't change the situation. If anything, it reinforced my impression that he was a pro. Buddy wouldn't have used him, otherwise. To keep his mind on other things, I said, "Will a car sit through a storm surge and still run?"

"Hotel parking lot."

I nodded as I walked.

"Storm tide. Storm surge is a misnomer."

"No kidding?"

"A surge is not governed by tide." He sounded pleased with himself.

I said, "I've learned something. Thanks."

There were more downed wires along the next cross street. An electric company van with portable ladders on its rack was idling at the far end, its driver looking down, either writing or typing something on a device. He would be a trouble man, there to mitigate risks. If there was something he could fix, he would.

The problems here were beyond his capability and most likely, he was calling in an order for a crew with a cherry-picker.

Buddy's Charger was parked in the next block, across and halfway down the street, facing us. Well beyond that was more trouble, another utility pole snapped off at its base. It tilted over the street, suspended at its top by the cable spanning its neighbors. A power line had snapped, and dangled from the broken pole, its free end lying in a loose coil on the wet asphalt. Some of the line lay under the water in the gutter that ran the length of the block.

The man seemed unconcerned. There could be an opportunity here. I said, "We should be careful. There's no telling what might be energized."

He kept on, guiding me with his hand on my arm, and said, "Relax, that's what it looked like when I pulled up." I heard a diesel engine, somewhere behind us, as we walked in the Charger's direction.

I wanted him focused on the downed wire. "You never know, man. It's still windy." I heard the vehicle's driver downshift as it neared us. I glanced back. It was a heavy derrick truck, its massive auger bedded. I supposed the new pole would be coming later. "If the live end of that wire has gotten blown into the water, there, the water's energized. That means the car could be live, too."

We were directly across from Buddy's Charger, one hundred feet shy of the downed wire. The cop said, "You're like my wife. You worry too much. Come on." He took a long step over the gutter between two ruined cars and pulled me along with him, waiting for the truck to pass, with his hand touching my arm. His other hand was still in his pocket, with his pistol.

The truck driver and passenger were looking past us, focused on the job ahead of them. I said, "It looks like it's arcing." He turned to look, and I shoved him into the truck's path. The impact knocked him three car lengths away.

I hurried to him and fished his keys free of his pocket. I heard both sets of truck doors open and close. "Oh, fuck," said one guy.

The other said, "He stepped right in front of me. You saw—there was nothing I could do. Jesus." He sounded ready to cry.

I spoke over them, not looking up. "He's still got a pulse. I'm a paramedic. My bag's in the car." I trotted across the street, unlocked the Charger and got in. Neither paid any attention to what I was doing, nor had they noticed the handcuffs. They didn't look away from the dead cop, even when I started the big Hemi. One had his arm around the other's shoulders as the engine burbled. I worked the shifter two-handed and took off. They noticed that. I saw their reflection in the rear view, watching me drive away. Even with the big engine winding out, I heard one yell, "Hey, where you going?"

I shifted and drove about four blocks in second gear, pulled over and undid the cuffs with the cop's key, and continued, over the bridge on Dorset, into Atlantic City proper. The cop had been about my size, so I didn't have to adjust the seat or mirrors. He'd been smart and left his phone in the console. It wouldn't do to have it ring at the wrong time. I hadn't time to get his wallet but reasoned it unlikely he had any of the thousand dollars I'd given Buddy on Wednesday. Or any of Buddy's wad. All told, I'd only netted two thousand dollars and change. After seeing Susan at the airport, I'd take Buddy's car to a chop shop on 29th Street. It should be worth three or four thousand, at least.

CHAPTER TWENTY THREE

I pitched Buddy's Easy Pass device out the window. I thought about the cameras at toll booths and considered wearing his coat but realized it wouldn't fool anyone who was looking at the pictures, and I didn't want to stop again. I certainly wasn't going back to Buddy's for my tools. There was probably enough time to make it to Philly International before Susan's plane left. Besides, Buddy's coat would be too long in the arms for me.

I didn't like taking the expressway. I was tethered to that fiasco last night until I got out of this car, but it was the only way I could make the airport in time.

I had to crank the radio to hear it over the Hemi. There was a lot of news coverage of the storm but also of the burglary and resulting fracas—no tally yet of those killed. The newscaster was calling it a mob war. I was hoping for word of flight delays but didn't hear any.

I had a bad moment. Buddy had been talking to a state cop. If there were others he was giving information to, it could mean a GPS somewhere in his car. I dismissed the idea almost as soon as it came. That cop had been in business for himself. He couldn't afford to play patty-cake with a guy who might be someone else's rat. He'd check. There wouldn't be a tracker in the car. I was tired but should have thought about all that, first.

Getting pulled over would be trouble but I pushed it, moving faster than Saturday morning traffic comfortably allowed for. I made good time, even stopping to pay with cash at the toll booths. By the clock on the dashboard, I was sure I'd be at the airport in time to talk to Susan. I didn't want her to leave.

I hit a jam a mile from the bridge. I stayed in lane, willing traffic to move. All the time I'd made was disappearing, the minutes evaporating as I inched along with the rest, the Charger's big cam turning over more slowly than it liked, the engine muttering. I threw on the flashers and bumped myself onto the shoulder, and accelerated, sounding the horn, flipping on the brights.

The delay proved to be a gaper gap, an accident on the far side of the median. Past that, normal traffic resumed. Horns blared as I pushed my way back onto the roadway.

When the bridge towers came into view, I thought about the mess I'd left back at the shore and what I'd heard about it now on the radio. Susan would hear or read all the same news. It would validate for her everything she'd said about me—the reason she was leaving.

The guy with the chop shop kept up with the news, too. If he heard about last night before I got there, once he saw Jersey plates, he wouldn't touch the car and he'd be annoyed that I'd come to him with it. If he heard about it after I'd gone, I'd have some money in my pocket, but I wouldn't be able to go back there. Neither choice was good. I couldn't just abandon the car somewhere in Philadelphia, either. Eventually, it would be recovered. If someone connected it to Buddy, having crossed a state line would make things federal. I didn't want the F.B.I. looking into this. Neither did I want to come back over the bridge and dump it in Jersey. The longer I was in the car, the more likely it was some cop would pull me over. Plus, it would take more time and I'd had enough of this outing.

I thumbed up a number on the cop's phone. After two rings, a man said, "Eastern Metals," loudly enough to be heard over the machine noises in the background.

"Could I speak to Flats?"

"Yeah." He must have put his hand over the receiver; I could hear a muffled yell. *"Yo, Flats."* A few seconds later, the man came back on. "He must be out in the yard, somewheres. Hold on a minute."

I waited almost two and Flats came on the line. "Yeah?"

I said, "I brought you a Chevelle last year."

He was quiet for a moment and said, "What do you want?"

"I got something else." I thought about time and said, "I'll be there in an hour or so."

"Is the trunk empty?"

"Of course."

"Don't of course me."

"I wouldn't bring you—"

"This as hot as that Chevelle?"

In the long run, it wouldn't pay me to bullshit this man, either. "At least that hot."

"One K."

"That's twice what I gave you last time."

"That was then, this is now. What do you want to do?"

"All right." I was too tired to argue. "One K is all right. I'll see you—" The line was dead. He'd hung up.

I couldn't be angry. I'd been careless. I pushed it hard, slowing again to pay the toll, picking it back up to mount the Walt Whitman.

At the top of the span, Philadelphia came into view through the suspension cables. The city was spread out below me. I could see past the distribution center, the stadiums, the navy yard property and idled refineries but the airport was too far away, and I couldn't see the tower. In the distance, an incoming jet circled slowly, making its approach. I glanced at the clock on the dash. I still had time. Coming off the bridge I let the Charger do what it could.

I parked short-term, next to a Honda like mine—the one I'd wrecked in the hotel garage last night. My reflection in the Charger's rear-view mirror showed red, tired eyes. I was stiff and felt sore walking through the lot. Raw. It felt like a year had passed since she told me she was leaving.

I crossed under the elevated line to departures and inside Terminal E. The last terminal was always least busy and made going through security easier. She'd told me that a while ago, before she knew that I didn't fly. Here, there were few TSA agents but also few passengers, pushing their belongings in plastic bins along the x-ray machine conveyors and walking shoeless through metal detectors. Most would be seasoned travelers, flying for work.

I checked the display for destinations and departure times. They progressed alphabetically, showing a dozen cities per screen, already past the Ms, so I'd have to wait to check for flights to Miami. When it got to the letter S, I saw she could fly to Saint Thomas with only a short layover in San Juan. That was the one. She'd mentioned the ferry to Saint John, once. Take-off was in ninety minutes, so she would need to get here soon. Unless she'd already gotten here and was gone.

There were seats in this part of the terminal, along its glass front but tired as I was, I didn't sit. My head was going in too many directions at once. The money. Minus the money I'd paid Buddy, I had two thousand and change. After the car crusher, a thousand dollars less. I shook my head. I had to get another car. And replace my hand tools.

Vehicles—cars, SUVs, buses—came and went, dropping people off and picking up others. A shuttlebus stopped, and a family of five got out, the father looking hassled, trundling too many bags, already tired this early in their journey, kids already bored, the mother on edge but comforting the little one who was whining.

I thought about what I was going to say. An electric shuttle cart carrying a big man with his leg in a cast beeped past me through the travelled area.

Susan got out of the back of a blue Tercel. I watched her thank the driver before she closed the door. She slung her pink backpack over her shoulder and came inside. Her eyes were puffy.

She headed for the escalator and didn't see me. I walked toward her. "Hey."

She gave a tiny start. "What the hell?" She took a step back and said, "You look like shit."

"Thanks."

She hesitated a moment before she said, more quietly, "I'm glad you're alive." Her voice was flat. Her face didn't give much away, either.

"I don't want you to leave."

"That town made national news last night." Before I spoke, she put up her hand and said, "I don't have time for your bullshit," and walked toward the escalator.

I said, "I'm done. Last night—I won't do that anymore. I'm finished."

Susan turned and looked at me, but her eyes showed no warmth. She said, "I've never heard you say that before."

I said, "I was thinking of you all night."

She stayed quiet a few moments and said, "Last night, watching the news, I was certain I'd never hear from you again. I—"

A car horn blared outside, and she looked. An Escalade had double parked and blocked another in. The driver popped on its flashers and got out of the car, held up a finger to the other driver. A guy wearing a suit that must have set him back three K got out of the backseat and the driver handed him a suitcase.

She looked back and said, "What will you do instead?"

"I'll do something else." She stared at me. I said, "I didn't even make money. I—"

"I don't want to hear about last night. I don't ever want to talk about any of this again." Behind her the Escalade drove off.

I nodded and said, "I'm done. I'll do something else." Susan was my best friend. My life was good. I didn't need this. "I can stop."

"I hope you mean that. You'd be good at anything you tried." She faced the escalator and looked back. There was a tiny bit of warmth showing in her eyes now. "I won't—" She cut herself off and looked away for a moment. She looked back and said, "Can you really stop?" Her voice choked on *stop*.

I nodded.

She gave me a look like the one she gave me when we'd first met, took her phone from her backpack and began tapping the screen. "I have to go—I promised Melissa—I couldn't cancel anyway. I'm already checked in." She looked up. "What if you come with me? I know you don't like to fly but could you come with me? Just come for the weekend. I'm not expected to start work until Monday."

I felt myself relax. Unspool might be a better word. "Yeah." I took a deep breath, let it out slowly and closed my eyes. I'd been unaware of how sore they were. I could do this. I rubbed them and said, "Yeah. That's a great idea." I had my legitimate ID. "I'll do that." Flying would put me in the TSA's database but it didn't matter. I was quitting. I could do this for her.

When I opened my eyes, Susan was occupied with her phone. She wore an earnest, pleased look on her face. "There's a flight later today. I'll get us a hotel room in Saint Thomas."

Past her, a Jaguar sedan stopped in front of the terminal doors. A couple got out of the back seat. They were tall and blond and looked like money.

Susan was working her way through the airline's site, poking at her screen. "There's a hotel near the ferry."

I looked outside. The man wore a comfortable, light tan suit; the woman a sleeveless blouse and slacks, a blue silk scarf tied to her bag. A necklace that probably ran four figures.

Susan kept at the phone. The couple's driver handled their luggage. They stood on the pavement, to the side of the terminal's sliding glass doors.

Buddy's Charger would show on security footage parking here the same day I took a flight in my own name. I'd have to take it to the crusher on Monday.

The guy outside took a gold cigarette case from his inside jacket pocket and lit up with a thin gold lighter. He didn't smoke like an addict, hungry for a last drag until his upcoming flight landed but seemed to be savoring it. With no expression on her face, the woman said something that made him laugh. Each sported an impossibly thin gold wristwatch. I thought of Buddy again and almost chuckled.

Susan said, "Yes, that's right." She was speaking to someone on her phone while wiping her eyes. "Yes, a two-night stay." She saw I was watching her and turned away, but I caught her smiling.

I smiled too and looked back outside. It was still gray, but I didn't care.

A Sky Cap was discussing something with the couple's driver. They weren't paying attention but neither seemed oblivious—just sure that someone they hired would handle anything necessary. I thought about Picozzi. These two didn't look anything like Charlie and his friend, Rita, but they vibed the same—a younger version. There was a hardness about them both, as though they made their money—together, probably—in some tough business, like strip clubs or chasing bad paper.

Finished, the driver nodded to them and drove away. The Jag had P-A tags and a local dealer's decal. The wind gusted. There wouldn't be many cars like it registered nearby. The man took a last drag on his smoke and snapped it away, pinwheeling sparks into the gutter.

Susan said, "You gotta be kidding me."

She'd seen me watching them. As the couple came inside through the sliding doors, Susan spoke to the call-taker, cutting him off. "I'm sorry, I've changed my mind." The couple walked past us without a glance.

"What's wrong?"

"I can't even feel angry." Susan put her phone in her backpack and looked at me with cold, sad eyes. "You can't help yourself."

It all seemed to hang there for a moment. I thought of things to say to her—that I had stared at the couple without intent, that it was reflexive behavior, a habit to be broken—but I only said, "I'm sorry, Susan." She'd seen more than me watching that couple. She'd seen *me*. I did, too.

She rode the escalator and was gone.

I walked back outside. With nothing documenting my presence here today, I could ditch the Charger in long-term parking after giving it a wipe. It might sit for weeks before anyone noticed. The state cop who killed Buddy claimed he'd already transferred its title. If the Charger had never been registered in Buddy's name, there would be nothing connecting it to me. I'd save a thousand bucks. It was something.

ABOUT THE AUTHOR

Tony is the author of the collection *Happy Hour and Other Philadelphia Cruelties* and the novels *Three Hours Past Midnight* and *A Few Days Away.*
He is a thirty-eight-year veteran of the Philadelphia Fire Department.